WALKING ON SUNSHINE

KRISTA LAKES

DARLA YORK

ABOUT THIS BOOK

There aren't enough hours in the day, and struggling single mom Jes just can't make it alone. Fortunately, a fantastic nanny just became available. Stacey is the perfect candidate: Young, college educated, with glowing references.

Trouble is, the nanny is a manny!

The last thing Jes expects is a tall, muscular, handsome stranger on her porch looking for work as a nanny. The last thing Jes wants is a new man complicating her life.

But Jes needs the help, and there's no one better for the job than Stacey "Cee" Cook. So she takes a chance and brings Cee into their lives. From beach trips to special meals to lacrosse games, Jes starts to feel like she has a family again. Soon sparks begin to fly, and she feels like she's walking on sunshine whenever Cee is around. But when his secrets threaten everything, can their love survive, or will it be nothing more than a summer fling?

Before I knew it he, was pulling me into his arms, closing them around me, the warmth in them spreading through my body. I looked up at him, and then he dipped down, his lips capturing mine.

He stole my breath with that kiss, and I lost all sense of time and place. I tried to steady myself, but he was there, holding me. Keeping me steady, making me fall at the same time. I hadn't had this feeling in years. It left me breathless and aching for more.

He pulled back to look at me. The only traces of the light violet in his eyes were on the outer edges. I felt like I was looking into the eyes of a wild animal, ready to take its prey. I wanted to be taken.

"I've been wanting to do that since you slammed the door in my face on that first day." He smiled at the memory, waiting for my reaction. I hadn't moved yet. The smile slowly started to fade.

"Cee..." I couldn't find any words to say. I was still shaking from the kiss, still lost in a whirlwind of emotion.

His own smile faded as he seemed to finally realize what was happening, what he had gotten caught up in. "I'm so sorry. I shouldn't have done that." He shifted from confident and lustful to unsure and respectful. "You're my employer. I don't want to mess anything up with Ben."

Every muscle in his body was tense. I gently grabbed his hand, to make sure he wouldn't run away. My head was still swimming from his kiss. I opened my mouth and could only make an inaudible grunting sound. My legs felt like Jell-O, and my insides were starting to burn with desire. That kiss had awoken something in me, a hunger that I let starve for years. Before I had time to let my thoughts cloud things, I let my body make my decisions for me.

I stood up and grabbed his head, pulling his lips down to mine. His body was stiff at first, his brain still trying to process what I was doing. He pulled back one more time to look me in the eyes. They had finally clouded back to that dangerous stormy color I yearned for so much.

"Cee..." I begged.

Before his name had finished escaping my lips, his mouth was back on mine...

Don't forget to sign up for Krista's newsletter! You'll be the first to see her new covers, comment on new books of hers, and always know when her books are available for free or on sale!

CHAPTER 1

My six-year-old son was missing.

I nearly dropped the phone on the restaurant table, my hand suddenly sweaty and weak, as I tried to process what the babysitter was telling me.

"I…I can't seem to find Ben," Charlotte repeated. Her voice was shaky across the cell phone connection. She started out slowly but her voice rose to panic midway through, and I knew she was back on track for a meltdown. "He asked me to grab a game from his bedroom, and when I came back down he was… he was gone. I've been looking everywhere trying to find him."

I took a deep breath, telling myself that this wasn't a disaster. If I stayed calm, everyone else would too. That was how things worked. Ben was fine. I swallowed hard against the lump quickly rising in my throat and the sour bile attempting to escape my stomach. *Stay calm.*

"It's okay, Char, I'll be there in a minute. Just keep looking and let me know if you find him. I'll start calling around, too." Ben had tried to run away before, but I was usually able to catch him before he got past the yard, curtailing his plans. This was the first time he took off when someone else was watching him.

"Thank you, Ms. Jes. I'm so sorry." I could hear her sniffling back tears.

"No, no, honey, it's fine. Stay calm and keep looking." I tried to keep my voice from wavering with worry. I didn't want to upset her even more. She needed to go out looking for Ben and if she was weepy, she couldn't do it. Ben was fine. He had to be.

Click.

I knew my son was usually responsible. He was a very bright six-year-old boy when he wanted to be, but I was more scared about the world around him. What if he had fallen and gotten hurt? Or worse, been taken? What if someone kidnapped him and was forcing him to do terrible things?

Breathe, I told myself. *He's probably just down by the old playground. He's fine.*

I almost believed myself.

I kept my head down, my eyes on my closed phone, and cleared my throat. I knew I was about to ruin the night out for my friends, but I knew they'd understand. They always did. "Ben's missing. I have to go find him. I'm sorry, ladies, I have to leave." My ears reddened from embarrassment. I always felt like I was the one everyone had to take care of like a child.

There was a silence as my three friends paused in their friendly banter and absorbed my words. This was supposed to be a fun evening where the four of us could sit and chatter about Tricia's fancy job, Melissa's latest hot date, Cindy's kids, and my horrible divorce.

But now my kid was missing.

"We'll come help," Cindy said without hesitation. "I'll call Ray. He'll get the kids together and start looking around their neighborhood." She began dialing her phone.

"I'll go grab the car right now," Tricia added as she pushed away her bar stool.

"I got the tab," said Melissa, already standing and heading to the bar with her wallet.

I took a shaky breath, trying to absorb the strength of my friends and keep from panicking. I wasn't alone in this. Divorced, but not alone. I didn't know what I would do without the three of them. They became my friends seven years ago when I first moved into their neighborhood, and they had never let me down since.

I called the phone that Ben's father and I had given him after the divorce. We had wanted to make sure he could always stay in contact with both of us, and now I prayed it was going to work. I knew it was pointless, though. Ben never picked up the phone. My heart skipped a beat with every ring, and when it went to his voice mail, I sighed, wishing it had been that easy.

Melissa, her jet black hair pulled neatly up and looking cool as a cucumber, touched my arm. I wished I could mirror her calm. She motioned to the door where Tricia had pulled up the car. They were waiting on me now. I grabbed my keys and hopped into the car with the other two women. With shaky hands, I nervously combed through my hair, fretfully pulling it into a bun as we drove home in silence. I could feel the panic bubbling up in my stomach as all of the worst-case scenarios started to pop up in my head.

Each minute that ticked by without a phone call from the babysitter saying that she had found him made me realize this was not one of his normal escapes. He had never been gone for this long. My son was the center of my world and I could feel him slipping through my fingers. He had to be okay. For both of us.

~

We turned into our neighborhood and rolled down the car windows. Warm, almost-summer evening air rushed in, carrying the scents of freshly cut grass and flowers. If I hadn't been looking for my son, it would have been a beautiful evening.

"Ben? Ben, where are you?" I yelled, trying to keep my voice from cracking with fear. There was no response. Just my voice echoing across the dark, empty yards. He wasn't here, or if he was, he wasn't answering.

Fear rose up and took over my mind as I imagined his face on a side of a milk carton, lost to me forever. I could feel the salty tears start to well up in my eyes, my composure slowly slipping away.

"Jes, Ray and the kids are coming down the other side of the street. They will let us know if they see anything," Cindy said, trying to distract me. I nodded, but my heart just kept sinking.

We continued to zig-zag back and forth through the neighborhood, making our way down the rows of identical houses. Every moment was agonizing.

Was that him? No, just a forgotten sweatshirt by a tree. Every misplaced toy, lost shoe or roving cat caught my eye. I noticed every movement, and at every inevitable discovery it wasn't him, my heart would sink just a little bit further.

Bicycles sat in driveways and I could see the children inside at kitchen tables eating dinner or watching just one more episode of TV before bed. That was where Ben should be. Not outside, running away from home.

The sun had set long ago and the world was lit by street-lamps when I finally saw him, walking on the sidewalk with his bike. Relief washed over me and I let out the breath I hadn't realized I'd been holding in.

"Ben!" I screamed, jumping out of the car before it had time to stop. "Ben, are you okay?" I practically flew over to him.

He turned toward me. "I'm fine, mom," he whispered. I wrapped him in my arms, his head hitting my chest. His bike clattered to the ground. I was sure he could feel my heart pounding through my light jacket. I clutched him in a tight grasp. Relief flowed through me, clearing my head of worry and replacing it with anger at the fear he caused me.

"What were you doing? You know it's dangerous to be out at night, and you don't even have a helmet. You should have told someone where you were going." I scolded him in a voice that wavered between anger and relief. My voice always gave away my feelings.

"I wanted to see Dad. I tried to text him, but he said he was too busy to stop by. So, I thought I could go to his house and say hi to him instead," he explained. His small face crumpled as he looked up at me, the question written all over his face even before he said the words. "Why doesn't he want to see me anymore?"

I released him from my grip, and gently pointed his head up towards me so I could look into his eyes. The redness above his cheeks built up into a mask of anger and grief, bringing out the blazing emerald of his eyes. Richard's eyes. His father's eyes.

His father who was never there.

The trail of one lonely tear made its way down his face and dropped onto his t-shirt in a little wet splash. It was proof of his pain, and it left me devastated.

I tucked the stray blond hairs behind his ears in an attempt to give myself time.

How would I explain to my son that his father had to leave because he broke my heart? How could I tell him that his father had found a new love and forgot everything else in the world?

"It's not that he doesn't want to see you, it's just that he's really busy." I released his face, and grabbed his hand as I slowly guided him to the car. I avoided his gaze as I told him the lie. It was a grown-up problem that he shouldn't have to understand. "We'll call him tomorrow, and then you'll be able to see him."

Ben followed behind me, hanging his head in silent defeat. He slid into the back seat as I grabbed his bike and tossed it into the trunk.

We all sat in silence as Tricia drove us to our house. It was nestled in a neighborhood of indistinguishable houses and manicured lawns. It still looked the same as it had the day I'd moved in with Richard eight years ago. The house matched all the nearby houses except for the bright blue door that I'd painted. I thought it added character to what seemed like a pretty drab color scheme of gray and brown. Richard thought it looked horrendous. After the divorce, I made sure to apply a fresh coat to the door each month to keep it bright.

I carried Ben past the kitchen and up the stairs to his bedroom. He was heavy in my arms, his sorrow weighing far more than his small frame. I was breathing hard by the time I made it up to the second floor. His room was the first one on the left, and the walls were covered in posters of sport stars and action heroes.

I laid him carefully into his twin bed, and tucked him into his sheets decorated with lacrosse sticks. As he snuggled down into a comfortable position, a soft smile crossed my face. He made that same snuggle motion when he was a baby.

I bent down to kiss his head. To me, he would always be my baby. But there was no doubt, he was growing up too fast, especially thanks to the divorce. I ran my fingers through his baby soft hair. His head was still hot from the day's activities and his cheeks were splotchy with tears. He leaned into my cool hand, and his eyes started to drift shut.

He was completely exhausted from his ordeal, both mentally and physically. I sat beside him, not saying anything, just stroking his hair and giving him silent reassurance that everything would be okay. When his breaths came out evenly, I carefully walked downstairs, avoiding the strewn clothes and random lacrosse balls that Ben had left out. Sitting at my dark wooden kitchen table was a fresh pot of coffee and my three girlfriends. They all looked up at me and smiled through their sympathetic eyes.

"How is he doing?" Cindy asked, slowly pouring me a cup of coffee.

"Exhausted," I replied, grabbing the cup and taking a sip. The hot liquid burned, but I needed the comforting taste. "He fell asleep the moment his head hit the pillow. I envy him for that. I wish I could lay my head down and conk out like that. I just don't know what to do with him. This is the third time he ran away, and now he's running away from the babysitter... Oh, no, the babysitter!" I looked around frantically, trying to find Charlotte.

"It's okay," Cindy assured me, patting my hand. "I had Ray take her home. She was pretty upset about the whole thing."

"Oh, thank you. I appreciate it. I just... I don't know what I would do without you guys." I sipped at the coffee. The bitterness matched my mood. "Ben has been getting worse after the divorce. I think it has to do with how little his dad sees him. He keeps coming up with excuses why he can't take

Ben. I think Ben's final breaking point was when I got this job. Maybe I should have waited a little bit longer."

"No!" They all chimed in at the same time. It still wasn't enough to keep me from feeling guilty.

"Jes, you've put your life on hold long enough. You seem so much happier now that you have something to keep you busy," Tricia explained as she refilled my cup.

"I just worry about Ben sometimes," I said, fiddling with my coffee cup. "He's still having problems with the divorce. His dad really doesn't come around anymore, and he's acting out in school. The counselors keep telling me that he's doing it for attention. But all Richard does is just spend more time with the bimbo."

Bile rose in the back of my throat as I thought about the woman who had replaced me. She was barely old enough to drink, and had an IQ that left me surprised that she'd managed to graduate middle school. The only thing that made her notable was her fiery red hair and boobs that would make Dolly Parton envious.

Before I walked in on her boinking my husband, she used to smile at me every time I came into the office, and she'd ask how Ben was doing. She even came into my house a few times, once when Richard threw an office BBQ. That entire time, as she was smiling at me, she was screwing my husband and destroying the life that Ben and I had. To say I hated her was an understatement.

"It's okay, Jes. Sometimes it's hard for men to handle two kids," Melissa informed me, a smirk slowly filling her face. "I mean if he leaves the secretary alone for too long, she might accidentally burn the house down with the toaster."

The bitter laugh that left me eased the ache on my heart a little bit.

Cindy looked thoughtful. "What about getting a nanny for Ben? I know with the summer months coming up, he'll have a lot of free time. I know a great service that might have what you need. I used them when Rose needed tutoring for college. I know they offer other services as well, nannies, babysitters, and people to do work around the house." She dug through her purse and found the card. "Give them a call tomorrow and they'll set you up with someone."

"Okay. I'll call," I said with the last bit of cheerfulness I could muster, and laid the card on the table. "Now, if you'll excuse me, I think I'm going to hit the hay."

We all got up and said our goodbyes. I hugged each of them close, grateful beyond words that they'd been there for me. I knew they loved me. I just always felt like such a mess compared to them. I wished having their hugs and words of support would be enough to satisfy this emptiness I felt, but I still felt like something was missing.

I shut the door behind them, locking it and watching out the window as they walked home. They were everything that I needed, but my heart screamed for something more. There was a hole in my heart where the life I had used to be. The more I looked back on it, Richard had never really filled that hole, but his betrayal only magnified how alone I really was.

I walked up the flight of stairs and got ready for bed. I shook my head at the sight in the mirror as I turned on the sink. Perched atop my head was a bird's nest of knotted hair, and crusted under my eyes were remnants of my eyeliner. *I really am a mess*, I thought.

After scrubbing my face and trying to run a comb through my hair, I gave up and fell on to my king-size bed. It was the same one that Richard and I had shared as a married couple. It was too big for me. It felt like I was lost in it. I used to have someone there, and now I was alone.

I put up with it because I hadn't been able to buy a smaller bed since the divorce. I did at least change the sheets to a bit more girly pattern. Dark purple sheets and a black and gray chevron bedspread now adorned the massive mattress. My ex-husband would have hated it, and that made me love it all the more. I set my alarm, thankful that tomorrow would be Friday, and Ben's last day of school. Things could only go up from here.

$\mathcal{I}$ woke up to a tug on my wrist, and squinted my eyes at the morning sun coming through my windows.

"Mom, it's time to go to school," Ben said gently. He stood next to my bed, dressed in a pair of jean shorts and a dark red shirt with his school's mascot, a panther in mid growl. "We're late. You slept through the alarm again."

I blinked my eyes a few times, trying to focus. The numbers on the clock blinked back at me with a gentle chirping. Somehow, the alarm volume had been bumped down and I never heard it go off.

"Oh no!" I yelled, jumping out of bed. We were late. Way late. My alarm clock said it was already eight o'clock. Ben was already supposed to be at school and work expected me in fifteen minutes. I sprinted to the bathroom and threw my hair up into a messy bun, thankful that it was casual Friday and I could get away with not looking my best.

"Hey, Ben, grab yourself a Pop-Tart for breakfast, and make sure to have your bag all ready," I yelled as I applied a quick sweep of blush and eyeliner.

"Can I have a soda too, Mom?" Ben called back as he left the bedroom.

"Yes, whatever you want, honey." I wasn't going to win the mother-of-the-year award today.

I quickly grabbed a pair of jeans and shimmied into them. When they didn't go over my hips, I fell on the bed to get a better angle to pull them on and sucked in every inch. I definitely needed to get a bigger pair, but these would have to do. I threw on the first top I found, and slipped on my sandals. As I hurried into the kitchen, I saw Ben sitting at the table with his Pop-Tart and orange soda.

"Okay, let's get to the car." I quickly filled my to-go cup with coffee and grabbed my own Pop-Tart. I glared at the hot pastry, knowing that the sugary and convenient little buggers were the reason why these jeans were a little snug.

"What's this, Mom?" Ben asked as he held up the business card from last night.

"Oh, thank you, honey." I shoved the card into my purse. "I was thinking of hiring you a nanny for the summer. Maybe someone who's old enough to drive."

Ben opened his mouth in protest, but before he could get a word, out I was pushing him to the door.

"Okay, let's go, let's go." I opened the door and let Ben scurry out, Pop-Tart in one hand, soda in the other. I grabbed his backpack and locked the door behind me.

We jumped into our silver minivan and pulled away. Eight fifteen. It was a going to be a rush for the record books. Ben's school had started at eight, so I had to walk Ben in to excuse his tardiness. We ran to the front door, and I brushed the remaining crumbs from Ben's Pop-Tart off his shirt.

"Head to class, honey. Let me sign you in. I'll see you once you're done with school. Love you." I gave him a kiss on the forehead, triggering a disgusted yuck from him.

The receptionist gave me a disapproving look as I quickly

jotted down my name on the sign-in sheet. I quietly ignored it and gave her a sweet smile to show how little I cared. *Judge me all you want, Ms. Manicure Nails and Curled Hair,* I thought to myself. *Not all of us have perfect lives.* I ran out the door and hopped back into my car.

The drive was smooth and I made great time. I snagged the last parking space and ran in to the office building. *Only a half hour late*, I thought as I checked my watch. I managed to catch the elevator in time and pushed the 5th floor button.

With a chance to finally take a breath. I checked everything in the mirrored doors of the elevator. I smoothed out my wrinkled blouse and did a little jump to pull my pants up a bit better over my hips. The image staring back at me did not make me happy. There was a slight bulge over my pants because they were too tight. My hair was no longer a messy bun, but a ball of dark hair with more hairs sticking out of it than in it. It wasn't until I looked down that I finally noticed I had picked two different sandals. *Ugh.* I stared at the mismatched pair, one black and one brown. I hoped no one would notice.

I made my way to my cubicle and sat down. I threw my purse under the desk as I powered up the computer. Since it was my first week, I hadn't decorated my office yet. I did have a photo pinned on the wall of Ben and me at the beach, right next to my calendar of dogs wearing funny outfits. This month it was a golden retriever wearing a letterman jacket and holding a sign in his mouth saying "School's out!"

I had printed off a few pictures of me and the girlfriends at a wine and chocolate tasting we did for my 35th birthday party, but after looking at them, I realized I looked a bit too tipsy to have them shown in the office. I didn't have any other pictures to put up on the walls. It was hard for me to decorate my office because Richard was in so many of my photos. He was the last thing I wanted to think about if I was having a rough day. He was the last thing I wanted to think about, period.

I unscrewed my coffee lid to pour in some more of the sugar and creamer I kept hidden in my desk.

Beep. The computer finished booting up as I sat the coffee next to my keyboard. *Time to get my day started*, I thought as I began answering emails and filling out reports.

Before I knew it, it was time for lunch, and I grabbed the protein bar stashed in my purse. As I yanked it out of the bag, crumpled receipts and old gum wrappers fell onto the floor. I shook my head at the trash. It really was a mess in that bag. Like my life.

With a sigh, I bent over and started to sort through it. Receipt, receipt, old gum wrapper, and finally the business card for the nanny Cindy gave me last night.

I really should call, I thought as I flattened the card out. Images of coming home to a clean house and cooked dinner started to fill my mind. At the very least, it would be wonderful having someone to help me out with Ben.

I examined the card closer. It was dark green with leaves embossed in the corners. "Season Services" was printed in bright gold letters, with the hours of operation underneath it. The place would be closing before I got out of work today, and the idea of having a moment to breathe when I got home was too good to pass up. My fingers dialed the number.

"Hello. Thank you for calling Seasons Services. Whether you need us for a reason or for a season, we are at your service. This is Megan. How may I direct your call today?"

"Hi, Megan. My name is Jes and I was given your number from my friend Cindy. She said you would be a great source for a nanny."

"Hi, Jes. Yes, we have many certified nannies that you can use. How old and how many kids do you have?"

"I have one son named Ben. He's six years old. His last day

of school is today, and I'd really like someone to look out for him while I'm at work." I slowly started to spin in my chair.

"We have a couple of people that would be a great fit for you. We can have one stop by on Saturday and see if that's what you're looking for. I have Stacey, who was just released from a prior nanny job when the family moved. They gave glowing reviews. Or I have Taylor, who has about a year of experience, but would be available only for part-time work during the next month. They are both Red Cross certified and have passed a thorough background check."

I thought about it for a moment. I couldn't do part time. "Stacey sounds like a good fit. I definitely need someone who is available full time."

"Wonderful. I'll need some more information about you so that Stacey will have it for tomorrow. Normally we have our clients fill out official applications, but we can just do this over the phone for you today and fill in the blanks later."

"Sure, sure." I continued to spin in my chair as I let her know about Ben, the hours I would need Stacey for, and my address.

"Okay, thank you, Jessica. That's all I need from you." I could hear her clicking keys on the computer through the phone. "Let me tell you a little bit more about Stacey."

My ears perked up, eager to know how wonderful my magical nanny was and what her specialties were. I felt my feet drag across the short carpet and gave a push with my foot to keep my momentum going. With the final push, my knee collided with the desk and knocked everything over. Coffee spilled everywhere.

"Oops! I'm so sorry to interrupt, I just spilled coffee all over my keyboard. I'll have to let you go." I scrambled to find a napkin or something to stop the flow of black liquid into the keys. "Have her come over at about eight AM. It will give me some time to chat with them."

"Sure, no problem, I'll send over Stacey's file tonight so you can have more details." The girl on the other line paused as she pulled up a file on her computer, oblivious to the coffee disaster I was experiencing. "I just wanted to let you know that Stacey is..."

I was sure that I saw smoke coming out of my computer, so I hastily hung up my phone before I heard anything else. This was a brand new work computer and it was still my first week. I coated the keyboard in tissues to try and absorb the liquid.

Ugh, this day can't end soon enough, I thought to myself. As soon as I finished mopping up the mess my office phone started to ring. I froze at the sound. Did they already find out about the mess I had made of my computer and were letting me go?

That phone made me nervous every time it rang. Taking a big breath, I picked up my phone and tried to answer it as calmly as possible.

"Hello?" I answered. My heart was hammering in my chest. *Please, don't let it be Ben's school. Please.*

"Hi, it's Steve. I just wanted to let you know that we found you a client to work with for next week."

I sighed with relief, plopping back into my chair. It wasn't my boss firing me and it wasn't Ben's school expelling him. My world wasn't about to end.

"Thanks, Steve. Have a great weekend." I wondered if he could hear the relief in my voice or if he just thought I sounded chipper. I hoped it was chipper.

"You, too," Steve said and then disconnected the call.

With the safety of knowing that I wasn't fired yet, I got back to work. The hours seemed to fly by as I allowed myself to daydream. I was excited that I'd finally have a set of hands to help me out with everything, and I imagined all the free time I would have. Maybe I would even be able to start dating...

No, not dating. I had swore off men. Just the thought of having to go through those awkward beginning moments put a pit in my stomach.

Hi, my name is Jes. I have a six-year-old son and I'm divorced. Have you seen my crazy life? Yes, that sounded so attractive to men.

The gym. That's what I would have time for. Then, I could actually fit in these pants again.

CHAPTER 3

The next morning started out in a rush. I had forgotten to wash Ben's jersey from the week before, and I was trying to get it dry in time for his match. Standing in my yoga pants and an oversized green-and-brown jersey with BEARS written across it, I fumed at the dryer. I was seriously considering just letting Ben wear my jersey, but he would have been swimming in it.

I pouted as I realized that I was swimming in it as well. My son's team had apparel that you could buy to support the team, and I didn't read the fine print and see that everything was in men's sizes. I had assumed it would all be women's because it was mostly moms taking their kids to the game.

I glared at the dryer one last time, then headed to the kitchen to throw some orange slices in a bag to bring as a snack for Ben. The doorbell rang, and I grinned. It had to be the nanny. My week, and Ben's summer, was about to get better. I wiped the sticky juice on my pants as I headed to the door.

"Hello," I said, opening up the door. I found myself facing a tall man with lean muscles. He looked to be in his early twenties and was wearing a tight white shirt that showed off his muscular chest. There was something about him that immediately made my heart flutter and my palms sweat.

He flashed a charming grin at me, which squinted the corners of his eyes. I realized they were a breathtaking violet. For a moment, I saw those eyes drift downward to my yoga pants. *He couldn't possibly be checking me out*, I thought. But just as quickly as I thought I saw it, his eyes snapped back to meet mine.

He had a green folder tucked under one of his delectable arms, which made me think he was trying to sell something. "Hi, my name is…" the man started.

"Mom, I need your help. I'm stuck!" Ben yelled. He barreled around the corner with his head stuck in the arm of his jersey.

"One sec, honey, there's a man at the door," I replied, trying not to laugh at his predicament.

"Mom, please! I can't breathe!" He sounded legitimately panicked.

"I'm so sorry, sir. I'm really busy right now, and I have to go help my son. Whatever you're selling or needing, I'm not interested. Have a good day."

I abruptly closed the door with my foot and turned to help my son try to get his head out of his armhole. It took a moment, but we got it. As soon as I finished getting his head out, he gave me a giant toothy grin.

He had chunks of cereal left in his teeth. I felt my gag reflex go a bit. "Go brush your teeth!" I scolded playfully.

Knock knock knock. I turned back to the door and opened it back up, getting frustrated with these constant interruptions when I was already running late.

"Hi. Ms. Hochs?" the man in the white shirt asked. This time, his eyes remained on my face, but I could swear that his eyes dilated a little.

"Hi, do I know you?" I asked, a little taken aback that such an attractive man would know my name.

"My name is Stacey. I'm the nanny from the service." He held up the green file, which had my name on it. His grin got even bigger.

"Oh. *OH.* My goodness. Stacey, I'm so sorry, I was expecting..." I stammered. I was embarrassed that I had assumed that it would be a woman nanny. My face flushed slightly.

"A woman?" He chuckled, making his eyes crinkle. "This isn't the first time someone thought that, and please call me Cee." He extended his hand for a handshake. I mirrored his motion, embarrassed, and was greeted by a calloused hand and a firm grip. His eyes were still on me, still fixated in a way that made me hot under the jersey.

I suddenly became very conscious of the fact that my hair was still dripping cold water down my back, and that the last time I put on makeup was over a day ago.

"Well, come in, come in. I'm so sorry, we're running a little behind for his game." I opened the door wider so that he could enter into my house.

I watched as he strolled in. He was tall, probably a good head and a half taller than me. I had to tilt my head up slightly to look into his eyes. He had a head of shaggy blond hair with hints of red in it that caught the morning sunlight and held the warmth. He moved confidently through the door, as if nothing could ever bother him.

As he walked in front of me, I smeared morning junk out of my eye, and gave my cheeks a pinch to add at least a touch of color to my pale complexion. My eyes drifted lower. His cargo shorts fit snugly around his waist and showed off his spectacular rear end. How the heck was this guy a nanny?

I quickly put my tongue back into my mouth, and tried to busy myself with Ben's lacrosse equipment.

"Can I get you anything to drink?" I asked, trying to keep

myself from staring for too long. I walked over to the sink to try and hide the array of dishes stacked on the counter. I thought my kitchen was spacious, but he seemed to fill the room. His eyes looked around, taking in the house in all of its messy glory. I grabbed a clean glass and walked toward him.

"No, I'm okay. I've got some water with me in the car. Is there anything that I can help you with?" I shrugged and went to put the glass back in the cupboard. When I turned around, I definitely saw his eyes on my ass this time. I felt my heart skip a beat, and I busied myself with my hair to make it look less like a damp rag hanging from my head.

"No, Ben should be down in a second, he's just brushing his teeth." As if on cue, we heard him thudding down the stairs.

"Hey, Ben, I want you to meet Stacey. He might be your new nanny," I said gesturing to Cee.

Ben looked confused. "But he's a boy," he whined.

"Ben, please introduce yourself and don't be rude. Nannies can be boys or girls, just like firefighters or nurses," I scolded.

He pouted his lower lip, but he walked over to Stacey and extended his hand.

"Hi, my name is Ben."

Cee smiled, crouched down to Ben's eye level, took his hand and shook it.

"Hi, Ben, my name is Stacey, but you can call me Cee," he said warmly.

"Hi, Cee." Ben responded quietly.

"That's a good job, Ben. Thank you," I praised Ben as he let go of Cee's hand. I looked at Cee and it dawned on me that I had scheduled the meeting at the same time as Ben's game.

"Would you be able to come with us to his game? I

completely forgot that I scheduled the interview at the same time as the game." I hoped my blush looked pretty.

"Not a problem," Cee replied, adding a smile onto the end of his words. *Good lord, the man had dimples. Sexy, sexy dimples.*

"Oh, thank you." I turned back to Ben. "Now, let's get in the car and head to your game. We don't want to be late again, like last week." I grabbed Ben's bag, and he snatched up his sticks and helmet. Cee opened the door so that we could both get through.

"Would you like to ride with us?" I asked turning to Cee as he made sure the door shut behind us.

"Sure," he said with a grin. The man's smile was positively electric.

He opened the back door of the silver minivan so Ben could hop in, and then walked around to the front of the car while I dropped the rest of the bags in the trunk. I turned to see Cee standing at the driver's door. He'd already propped it open for me.

"Oh, thanks," I said, slightly taken aback. I couldn't remember the last time someone opened a door for me, let alone the driver's side door. I could count the number of times on one hand Richard had been a gentleman and opened any door for me.

As I got in, Cee used his hand to guide the small of my back into the car. Goosebumps trickled down my arm at his touch.

He's just being chivalrous, I told myself. *Nothing to get excited about.* Yet the goosebumps from his touch remained.

I got in and he carefully shut the door behind me. He walked around the front of the car and I tried not to check out his ass as he walked, but it wasn't easy. I kept missing the ignition and couldn't get the key in until he was at his door.

He slid easily into the passenger seat and put on his seat

belt. "You all buckled up?" he asked, turning back to check in with Ben.

"Yup," Ben responded, playing with a lacrosse ball in his hands.

I put the car in reverse, and started the drive toward the field.

CHAPTER 4

"So, Cee, tell me about yourself. I really haven't had any time to look at your profile," I admitted.

"I've been a nanny for a few years. I'm originally from Arizona and moved out here for college. I'll give you my resume once we get back to the house. My last job was the Jones family. Do you know them?"

I shook my head. "No."

"Well, they lived about two miles away from here, not too far. Same school district. I watched their kids Dana and Michael. Michael is about Ben's age now. Anyway, the family moved to Chicago for work."

"That's too bad," I said, glancing over at him. I could tell from the look on his face that he had really cared about them.

"Yeah, they asked me to come with them, but I love California too much to ever leave the beach. I have their number on my resume if you need to check references."

"Okay. Thanks." I knew I would never call them, but I liked that he offered up the information. Cee intrigued me. "Where did you go to school?"

"I went to California State University," he answered proudly.

"And you're from Arizona? Out-of-state tuition must have been expensive!" I wasn't sure why, maybe it was because I'd just started tracking my own finances, but it popped out of my mouth. I bit down on my tongue. So much for making a good impression.

"Not really," he replied with a casual shrug that made me feel less awkward. "I got through it on an athletic scholarship. Lacrosse, actually."

"What position did you play?" Ben chirped in at hearing the word lacrosse.

"Ben, you know what I said about interrupting when people are talking," I scolded, staring back at him in the rear view mirror.

"Sorry, Mom," Ben apologized, but his face said he was more excited about what Cee had to say than manners.

"Well, Ben, I played midfielder. What position do you play?" Cee asked as he turned in his chair to get a look at Ben.

"I'm goalie right now," Ben said as he beamed with pride.

"That's a hard position. I used to play that when I started high school. How long have you been playing that position?"

"This is my first season playing on a team. Before that, it was just me and Jake throwing the ball around with his dad. He knows a lot about this stuff."

"Well, I'm excited to see you play today. Maybe afterward, I can give you some pointers." His voice sounded genuine with the proposition.

I smiled as I watched Ben in the rear view mirror. For the first time in weeks, his eyes lit up, and I knew that Ben had already decided that he wanted Cee to stick around. Anyone who would talk to him about lacrosse was golden in his book.

"We're here," I said as I parked at the field. The five fields spread out before us, almost big enough to get lost in. Two fields were set up for soccer games and the other three were ready for lacrosse. There was a little jungle gym nearby for smaller kids as well.

Ben hopped out of the car and I popped the back door. He grabbed his bag and ran to the field to join the others, who were already tying up their cleats.

"We have about twenty minutes until the game starts up. Do you want to grab some coffee? It'll give us more time to get acquainted," I said. I shut the trunk and turned to look up at Cee. A thrill went through me as I looked up into his eyes. I was finally able to give those eyes the attention that they deserved. They were endless and possibly the most beautiful thing I had ever seen.

Stop it. He's your nanny, I chided myself. The nanny was the last person on the planet I should be admiring for his physical characteristics.

"Sure, as long as I get to ask some questions too," Cee said, a hint of humor creeping into his voice.

We headed to the coffee stand just across the road, walking at a leisurely pace. It was a little drive-up food truck, that offered breakfast burritos and coffee to the players' parents. I grabbed my basic Americano, while he just got a cup of coffee with some cream.

"Tell me a little bit more about Ben," Cee said, taking a sip of his coffee. His violet eyes were fixed on me, looking at me like I was the only interesting thing he saw.

I brushed a strand of hair out of my face, knowing I was about to smile. I always smiled when I talked about Ben.

"He's six years old, and the only thing that interests him is lacrosse. Watching it, playing it, or reading about it. I think he loves it more than he loves me some days," I explained, thinking that the only time he'd gotten that ear-to-ear grin in the last few months was when he was playing.

"He sounds like most six-year-old boys," Cee said, chuckling. When he smiled, the dimples deepened, making him even more handsome. "I remember when I was that age. If it wasn't sports or action figures you were S.O.L."

I nodded, knowing the feeling of being S.O.L all too well. The conversation fell quiet for a moment as we both sipped on our drinks. I opened my mouth to ask a question, but every time I did, my mind went blank. His good looks just seemed to wipe my mind of thought. The pause was slowly turning awkward.

He finally cleared his throat and asked, "So, how did you come to need my services?"

I sighed, glad that he'd finally broken the silence, even if it meant I had to explain my train-wreck of a life.

"I went through a divorce about a year ago, and started a new career last week." The words were simple, even though the reality was hard. I shrugged, trying to move the guilt weighing on my shoulders.

"It must've been hard." He took a slow sip of coffee, his beautiful eyes never leaving my face. I felt as if the world revolved around me when he looked at me like that.

"It's been tough on Ben. I think if he has someone to look out for him, an adult he can rely on other than me, it would be good for him." I looked out at the field where the boys were getting ready to play and my heart ached for my son. "Especially with summer starting, he'll have a lot of free time. I don't want him to look back on his childhood as a terrible time."

"I'm sorry to hear that. I'll definitely keep him busy if you want to keep me on. I know the whole male nanny thing is a turn-off to some people." He shrugged his muscular shoulders and grinned. "But I'm pretty good at it."

Ha, turn-off? I thought. *I would say it's a turn-on.* I shook my head, trying to clear the thoughts of what he would look like turned on out of my brain. *No, I was not going to start looking at men now. Especially one who's this young, and shouldn't be tied down by a woman with baggage.*

A whistle blew in the distance, signaling the beginning of the lineup and saving me from being inappropriate with our new nanny. "It looks like the game's about to start. Let's head over to the field."

We walked to where the other parents stood watching their children. Some of the lacrosse moms gave a wide-eyed stare at the attractive stranger I brought to the game. It wasn't every day a guy like this was on the field. Normally the field was dotted with middle-aged men with beer bellies and growing bald spots. Cee was anything but that. I just smiled politely, trying to ignore their burning eyes, but I knew my cheeks were red.

We found a good spot near Ben's goal and took a seat. It wasn't until I realized that the grass was still damp with dew that I regretted the decision. I jumped up and tried to pull down my oversized jersey to hide the wet spot blossoming across my ample rear-end. It wasn't working very well. Cee smiled and offered his hand to hold my coffee while I struggled. I swore I heard a low chuckle from him, but when I looked at him, he had already turned away.

I pulled up my yoga pants a little higher and folded them over, hoping to minimize the wet on my butt as much as possible. I was still hoping to make a decent first impression on the hot guy.

I rolled my eyes at myself. *With moves like this, I am destined to be alone,* I told myself, knowing it was true. By the time I felt decent, the whistle blew and the referee dropped the ball into the face off.

The other team, the Blue Jays, won the face off, and the

kids sprinted down the field. I watched Ben as he fidgeted nervously, watching the players come toward him. A few more back and forth passes between the opponent, and BAM, the ball soared past Ben's head. Goal. I heard cheers from the Blue Jays' parents. Ben dropped his head in defeat. It was going to be like the last game all over again.

I yelled out and clapped. "It's okay, Ben, it was a lucky shot. We'll get them next time." I hoped that the early score wouldn't completely destroy his confidence.

Ben got the ball out of the net and threw it to one of the kids on his team. Cee and I watched as the kids passed the ball with ease. I took my eyes away from the game and glanced at Cee, figuring that I wouldn't be caught. I was right. He was sucked into the action of the game. His dark violet eyes tracked the ball and his strong chin was clenched in a hard line. I told myself I was just looking so that I could recognize the man who would be watching my son, but I knew I was really just ogling.

An older couple came to sit beside us and Cee scooted closer to met to give them room. Our knees knocked slightly, pressing together as I absentmindedly moved over. My breath caught, but he was really focused on this game. Every once in a while he muttered to himself, and I picked up a "that was a foul... oh man, ref, come on..." I chuckled a bit, realizing how much he really got into this sport. He would be perfect for Ben.

I kept my knee pressed against his, enjoying his warmth, even if I knew I would never, and could never, have anything more.

I heard cheering from our side and clapped absentmindedly, still wrapped up in watching Cee's reaction to the game. I had never seen anyone so interested before. At the few games my ex-husband attended, Richard would cheer occasionally, but never quite like this. He was still sore that Ben never wanted to play football, and become the star quarterback like his dad. He never gave lacrosse this much attention.

It wasn't long before the ball was back on Ben's side of the field, and the opposing team scored again. And again. And then some more. My ears started to ache for the halftime whistle so that Ben could take a break from this. Like sweet music, the whistle blew before the Jays could score again on Ben. It was the end of the half and the score was 6-3. Our team was losing, and I knew Ben felt it was his fault. The kids all ran off the field and grabbed their water bottles from their parents.

"Hey, Ben," Cee called as Ben walked over. "You're doing really great. This is a hard team to be up against. Can I give you advice, player to player?"

"Sure. I don't know what it'll do though." Ben shrugged, taking a sip out of his water bottle. Defeat hung in his eyes, and he refused to face Cee, who knelt in the grass before him.

"I noticed that when a person comes at you with the ball, you look the guy straight on and try to guess where the ball will go. Try to point your thumbs at the guy carrying the ball and follow his movements." He grabbed the lacrosse stick laying on the ground and showed him what he meant. "That helps you see the shot and put your stick in the right spot. Does that make sense?"

Ben nodded slowly. "Yeah, I get it. So I look like this as the shot comes?" Ben picked up his stick and angled it.

"Perfect! And shuffle your feet to help follow the shooter as well." Cee stood up into a hunched squat and moved his feet diagonally along the grass, away and back again.

"Got it," Ben said, grinning up at Cee, the words clicking in his brain and giving him hope for the next half. "Thanks." Ben ran off to the coach as the team gathered to talk before the start of the second half. It looked like the pep talk had re-energized Ben.

"Wow, you really know what you're talking about. I'm impressed." I smiled at Cee.

"Well they don't give out lacrosse scholarships for good looks," he replied with a smirk. I giggled, wishing I didn't feel quite so much like a high school girl for laughing at a cute guy's joke.

As he stood upright, Cee wiped the wet grass from his knees. We crossed to the other side of the field to watch the second half of the game. The early morning cloud cover had cleared, and as we walked over the damp grass, the warm sun triggered a trickle of sweat down my back.

Ben had taken his position in between the goal posts, and started to practice the advice that Cee had just given him. The whistle blew and the face off began. The other team got the ball and started to barrel down the field. Ben was watching the guy come in, and wasn't moving as the guy started to come down the right side.

"Shuffle those feet," Cee shouted, cupping his hands over his mouth.

Ben gave a slight nod and started shuffling his feet, looking at the shooter with his thumb in front of his face.

The ball whizzed through the air and for a moment I was sure Ben was going to miss it. I held my breath and waited.

"Wahoooo!" I cheered as he saved the ball in the net of his lacrosse stick with ease. He threw the ball to one of his team-mates, who carried it to the other side.

Ben was smiling so wide I could see it through his helmet. I didn't think I'd ever seen him so excited.

Cee was already having a positive effect on my son. The coaching that he'd given to Ben in just a few minutes had already made a difference. Cee was making a difference. If I had any doubts about Cee, this cleared them. Cee was perfect for Ben.

I couldn't believe it when the whistle blew signaling the end of the game and the final score was 6-7. The Bears won, and Ben didn't let a single ball get by him in the second half!

CHAPTER 5

en ran off the field and I caught him up in a big hug. He was practically vibrating with excitement and I couldn't be happier for him.

"You did such an amazing job!" I beamed with pride.

"Thanks, Mom. It was all thanks to Cee." He held out his hand for a high five and Cee happily returned it.

"I think it's time to celebrate. Who wants breakfast?" I asked, putting Ben's equipment in the bag as he shed off each pad.

"Yes! Can Cee come too?" Ben pleaded.

"Of course he can. He deserves a reward too for the great advice he gave." Not to mention he was easy on the eyes and fun conversation. I grinned, putting Ben's stick in the bag and zipping it up. I went to lift the bag, but before I could, Cee grabbed it.

"I got this," Cee said. He lifted the bag into the van as if it weighed nothing.

"Thanks." I smiled. I could get used to this help, not to mention the package it came in.

I definitely missed having an extra set of hands around.

We chose to have breakfast at the Morning Rise, a fantastic little breakfast place that had the best crepes in town. I sat quietly, eating my strawberry crepes and sipping on my Americano, while the two boys talked about lacrosse. I didn't have much to add to the conversation, but it was nice to see Ben so excited to chat with someone, and Cee kept Ben enthralled with his knowledge of sports. I didn't care that I barely got a word in edgewise.

I had to keep interrupting them so they'd actually take bites of their pancakes before they went cold. They'd both ordered chocolate chip pancakes with whipped cream. As I watched them eat, I could feel my heart becoming lighter. There was a future here, a future where Ben was happy and taken care of. This could be a man who could give him the attention he needed. He could be the fix that was required all along. I couldn't help but notice how good they looked together as Cee demonstrated maneuvers with the saltshaker.

Don't get ahead of yourself, I reminded myself silently. *He's just Ben's nanny. Nothing more. That's all he'll ever be, so don't go thinking they look like family.*

Ben didn't stop grinning during the entire meal. They were already fast friends, and I knew that Ben would be happy and safe with Cee. My decision, it seemed, was made up for me. Cee would just have to stay on.

After two more cups of coffee and a finished plate of crepes, I finally had to drag the boys away from the table or they would have kept talking for hours. It was cute, and normally I would have encouraged it, but we had errands to run.

When we got back to the house, Cee brought in all the equipment for me before I even had a chance to lift it. Handsome and nice. A winning combination.

"This was awesome, Cee. Thank you so much." Ben

grinned one last time before turning to head up to take his shower. "I can't wait to see you on Monday."

"I guess that decision was made for me," I said with a chuckle. Cee leaned gracefully against the kitchen doorway, watching Ben sprint up the stairs before turning to look at me. A shiver ran through me as his violet eyes caught mine.

"So, I got the job?" Cee asked with a smile, giving me a wink.

"Yes, you were wonderful. I can't believe how quickly Ben has taken to you." I shook my head and started to unload Ben's equipment to air out. "It's so good to see him connecting with a man. With his dad staying out of the picture, it's been really rough on him."

"Ben's such a great kid. I couldn't think of anyone not wanting to hang out with him," he said, shaking his head in disbelief. He started to sort through the green file on the counter and pulled out a piece of paper.

"I think you'll be a good influence on him," I said softly. I looked up to find his violet eyes on mine, and my heart started to pound. I knew I shouldn't have that kind of reaction to a man at least ten younger than me. It just wasn't appropriate.

He was in high school when you were getting married. That thought calmed my racing heart real quick.

"Jes, it's been a pleasure to talk with you today. Here's my resume. I look forward to working here and spending time with your son." He smiled professionally, placing the paper in my hand, and I knew the increase in heart rate had to be entirely on my end. I was just an old woman to him. "If you need anything, please feel free to call me at this number." He wrote down his number on the pad I used for grocery lists. "I'll see you Monday before you leave for work. "

I walked him to the door and watched as he walked to his car. *Man, that guy really has a glorious ass.* I shook my head to clear the stupor it left me in and shut the door. Staring at his ass was so wrong, and yet so right.

My pocket started to vibrate. With a sigh, I pushed the image of Cee's butt out of my mind and answered my phone.

"Hi, This is Megan from the Seasonal Service. How are you doing today?"

"Good, thanks. How are you?"

"Wonderful. We just wanted to follow up on the interview. We just received a text from Cee notifying us that you would like to bring him on."

"Yes, he was fantastic," I agreed. "I would definitely be interested in having him as my full time nanny."

"Perfect, Ms. Hochs, I'll mark him down as being hired in the system," she replied. I could hear the tap of keys on the other end.

"Thank you so much." I clicked my phone shut and peeked one last time out the window, but Cee was already gone. I couldn't wait for him to come back.

The rest of the weekend flew by, and I couldn't do anything without hearing something from Ben about Cee. He couldn't stop talking about how great he was, how strong he was, and how much he knew about lacrosse. I was fairly sure Ben made some of it up, because there was no way he could know from just a couple of hours together that Cee could lift 500 pounds or could make a shot on a goalie completely blindfolded. Still, I loved his enthusiasm.

I was almost thankful when Monday morning came so I could get away from him constantly talking about his nanny. As I got ready for my morning, there was a tap at the door downstairs. I had just finished putting eyeliner on my right eye and placed it on the sink. I closed my ratty purple robe and hurried downstairs to the door.

I opened the door and instantly regretted not thinking about what I looked like. Cee was standing there in a pair of board shorts and a V neck T-shirt that showed off his smooth chest. He had two cups of coffee in his large hands. My mouth hung open slightly as I took him all in with the morning light. I really needed to learn to start putting myself together before he arrived. Seeing him made me aware of how disheveled I looked.

"Hi, Jes, how are you today?" He smiled, exposing his perfect grin and cute dimples. He had somehow become more attractive in the last few days.

"I'm good, come on in. How about you?" I stepped back so he could come inside. I swallowed hard, regaining my composure, and tightened the threadbare robe around me as best I could.

"Good. Here, I brought this for you. Americano, right?" He handed me one of the coffee cups.

"Yes, thanks." I took the coffee cup and had a long sip. Perfection. I couldn't believe he remembered the way I took my coffee after just one day. If he wasn't so much younger than me and not my son's nanny, I would have married him on the spot.

"Is Ben up yet?" Cee asked looking around.

"Yeah, he's getting dressed now." I raised my eyes to the ceiling as I heard Ben moving and stomping upstairs.

"Okay." Cee raised his eyebrows as a loud crash that sounded like a pile of lacrosse sticks falling came from the ceiling. He chuckled. "Would you mind if I make breakfast for you guys?"

I nearly spit my coffee out. Not only did he bring coffee, but he made breakfast too? "If you want. We normally just have some cereal or I grab a bar. You really don't have to."

"Hey, it's what I'm here for. And it's always good to make a great impression on the first day. Never know what the boss is thinking." He flashed his smile again, crinkling his violet eyes as he made his way to the kitchen. For a moment, I thought there might be something more to his words about impressing the boss, but I knew that couldn't be right. There was no way I was even on his radar.

Still, as I went back upstairs to finish getting ready, I

thought about other ways he could make a good impression on the boss. I pushed the thought away. There would be time to fantasize later.

"Hey, Ben! Cee is here," I called, knocking on Ben's door as I passed.

"Yes!" Ben yipped in excitement, and darted past me on the landing, nearly knocking me over. I went back to my bathroom and finished getting my hair done and putting my makeup on. I put extra attention on trying to pick out my outfit. I didn't want Cee to think I was a total slob after seeing me in only a robe or a giant jersey.

I grabbed a pair of black trousers and a silk top that was a bit more formal than what I would normally wear to a regular a day at the office, but what the heck. A girl didn't need a reason to look nice.

The pants were a little tight, but they still looked good. I smoothed my hair, suddenly anxious of what Cee would think. I knew it shouldn't matter, but somehow it did. I wanted to look good for him. I glanced one last time in the mirror and flashed myself a grin. I looked good. I headed back downstairs and the heavenly scent of bacon and eggs hit me.

"I didn't even know I had bacon left," I said looking at the plate waiting for me on the kitchen table. It looked amazing.

"Yup. Found it under the squash…well, what was left of the squash, anyway. It kind of looked a bit more liquid then what I'm used to." Cee poured me a glass of orange juice as I took a bite of scrambled eggs. The eggs were perfectly cooked, with a hint of salt and pepper.

"Yeah, I probably should clean that out. We've been eating out a lot more than what we're used to." I looked at the clock and nearly choked on my eggs. *Oh, no.* I was late for work. Again. I quickly stuffed a couple more bites of eggs in my mouth and grabbed the slices of bacon.

"I've got to go. I'm running late. I'll see you when I'm done with work at about 5. If you need anything, please give me a call." I started to look around for a pen and paper, feeling jumbled. "I'll leave you my number."

"It's okay, Ms. Hochs, I already have it. Remember that questionnaire you filled out when you first started looking for a Nanny? They gave me all the information. We can discuss what your plans look like for the rest of this week and month later tonight."

"Thank you," I said appreciatively. I was glad I had someone who was organized to help me out. "I'll see you tonight and I'll text you when I can at work, just to check how things are going."

I kissed Ben on the top of his head, ran out the door and jumped into my car, feeling like I'd had a weight taken off my shoulders. It was so nice to have a pair of hands who could cook, help with chores and, most importantly, spend time with my son.

I was excited when I drove home after a long day at work. I couldn't wait to hear about what Ben and Cee did today. I parked in the driveway, and as I grabbed my purse my phone started buzzing. It was Richard. Melissa had helpfully renamed him "The DICK" on my phone. I took a big breath. He didn't call me often.

"Hi, Richard," I answered flatly. I knew he was about to yell at the request I'd made a few weeks ago, asking him to pay for half of Ben's lacrosse camps over the summer. I'd been waiting for this call for a week.

"Jes, what the hell is this? You want four hundred dollars for him to do what?" Richard screamed over the phone.

I felt my heart beat start to quicken. I always hated getting in fights with him.

"I just thought you wanted to help out. You said you would support him in sports he wanted to play." I thought I managed to sound calm and reasonable and was rather proud of myself.

"Yeah, a *real* sport like football. What are they going to teach him, how to run without tripping over his own two feet?" He gave a slight chuckle at his own joke. I was glad he couldn't see me rolling my eyes at him.

"Richard, we've talked about this. Ben really likes lacrosse. I want to support him in the sport he likes, not the one you pick for him." I tried to make my voice firm, but I felt it quaver. The thought that Richard didn't want to support Ben because it wasn't football made me realize how juvenile my ex-husband could be.

"There is no way in hell that I am going to help pay for this. They're all trying to scam people out of all their money for a crap sport that no one cares about." His voice rose to the tone that always made me feel weak and unimportant. "I pay the child support, and I won't pay a penny more for ridiculous shit like this."

"Richard, please..." But all I heard was a dead tone on the other end. The bastard had hung up on me.

I felt my blood boil, and it wasn't about the money. He hadn't asked about Ben at all. All he cared about was the money. My breath caught in my throat as I kept back burning tears. I yanked my hair up in a tight bun and took a few deep breaths. I was not going to let this ruin my day, and I did not want to have anyone see me upset. Especially not Cee.

With one last wipe under my eyes, I walked through the door to the smell of rolls and baked chicken. Cee and Ben were sitting on the living room floor with lacrosse sticks in hand.

"Now, take this string and loop it around here, and attach it to your basket. Nice, and knot it here. See, that's the first step in learning to tie your stick. We'll have to continue later because your mom is home. I don't know about you, but I'm starving," Cee said, standing up.

He got up and stretched, and his shorts rose up, showing his toned legs. My face flushed slightly as I caught myself staring at him.

"Now go say hello to your mom, and tell her all about your day. I'm going to finish getting dinner ready," Cee instructed Ben. He looked over and smiled. "Hi, Jes. I hope chicken and rice with baked rolls sounds good to you. Ben said it's his favorite."

"Oh, my gosh, yes. That sounds amazing." I plopped my bag down and tossed my shoes in the corner. It felt good to be home. Having Cee here already felt natural and right. The fight with Richard was becoming the furthest thing from my mind.

"Mom, look what Cee taught me today!" Ben ran over to show me a half-strung lacrosse head. "He says it'll take a lot of practice, but I can do it myself one day, and then I can switch out different colors."

"That sounds awesome, Ben," I told him with an eager smile as I admired his handiwork. It was so nice to see him excited and glad. "Now go sit down at the table so we can eat."

Cee dished up steaming chicken smothered in a mushroom rice sauce onto the places, and put the warm rolls in a bowl in the center of the table. I nearly cried with joy. From a bad phone call to this. I had died and gone to heaven. It was silly and simple, but for the first time in weeks, both Ben and I were happy. All because of Cee.

"Ben, can you put the jam and butter out? Then we can get dinner started," Cee told Ben. I sat at the table in awe as Ben got up and grabbed the items willingly.

"Who are you and what did you do with my son?" I said jokingly at Cee. "It's usually like pulling teeth to get him to do anything."

"Just one of my many secrets, I guess." Cee replied with a smile. I could have kissed him, I was so happy.

Dinner was one of the most delicious meals I'd eaten in years. After so many bad frozen dinners, and my many failed attempts at cooking, it was an amazing change. It reminded me of my mom's cooking. I felt warm and safe, a feeling that I hadn't had in ages.

"This is incredible. How did you learn to cook like this?" I shoveled another bite into my mouth, hoping I didn't look too greedy.

"I've always liked to cook, and at one of my previous gigs, the kids were getting sick of PB&J, so I pulled out a few of my mom's old recipes." Cee played with his spoon and didn't look up from his bowl, despite the compliment. He seemed to be almost ashamed. "It kind of stuck after that."

"Tell your mom she's amazing. I'll have to steal the recipe from her sometime." I smiled warmly, wondering what kind of a woman raised someone as charming as Cee.

"Yeah, she was," Cee said, staring into his plate uncomfortably. The easy charm disappeared for a moment, obviously grieving the loss of his mother. After a moment, he cleared his throat and looked over at Ben. "Hey, how 'bout you tell your mom what we did today?"

I listened to Ben, but my attention was on Cee. He played with his food, pushing the chicken around in the sauce as if he were trying to make it disappear without eating it. I felt a low ache in my chest at his obvious grief.

"We went outside and played lacrosse for awhile," Ben

babbled, barely pausing to breathe in between his sentences, he was so excited. "Cee taught me some sweet new moves to use for my next game. Then we had lunch. And then we went outside and just threw the ball around. And then we came back inside and started on dinner. Cee was showing me how to string the lacrosse stick." He had a grin on his face, but his eyes were starting to droop.

CHAPTER 7

*B*efore long, Ben looked like the toothpicks holding his eyelids open were breaking.

Cee obviously noticed as well. "Ben, you should go get ready for bed. Your mom and I have to talk about business, which is super boring."

"You don't have to tell me twice," Ben said, sliding out of his chair. He paused, his big green eyes going to Cee and looking worried. "You'll be back tomorrow, right?"

"Of course I will," Cee promised. "I have to finish teaching you how to do those laces."

The worry vanished from Ben's face, and the light that I loved so much shone out from them again. Even though we'd only known Cee for a couple of days, I knew that Cee could see it too, and that he would fight just as hard as I did to keep it there.

"I'll be up to tuck you in after Cee leaves," I called to him as he dragged himself up the stairs.

Cee took a file from his bag that had my name and Ben's name on it. He handed it to me and our hands touched. A flash of heat went through me, but Cee moved nonchalantly. Apparently, he didn't feel the same spark.

"Here's the contract agreement that the agency needs you to sign. I'd also like to talk about how you'd like things to be run with Ben. I know that when you're at work, I'm in charge, but I want to make sure that I try to mirror what you normally do, so that Ben is happiest." He cleared the table of the dirty dishes as I looked over the paperwork.

I thumbed through the stack of papers. "Wow, this is so official. I didn't have any idea it was this in-depth."

"Some of it's legal documents, in case I can't get in touch with you, or Ben gets hurt. Some of it's mine as well. It's just schedules that I like to keep for my personal time ," Cee explained, putting the dishes in the dishwasher.

"The first page is the basic information about me, my references, cell number, certifications, as well as my home address, just in case you need to drop Ben off at my place. I would prefer not to have that, but I know with errands or work schedules, things might get a bit hectic." He walked over to the table and stood behind me, leaning over my shoulder so he could point to something on the page. He didn't touch me, but I could feel the heat of his body on my back, and my own body trembled in response.

I could smell his cologne. He smelled of warmth and grass. It was intoxicating. I inhaled deeply, etching the smell into my memory. I didn't know it was possible for a man to smell this good. It didn't seem fair.

"Now, here," he explained, pointing to the page. His body grazed my shoulder, his touch sending electric heat surging through me. He held still for a moment, his finger hoovering just above the page. "This is just agreements of hours, and duties. I'm assuming you'll want me Monday through Friday for your normal working hours, eight to five?" He moved away and sat down in the chair next to me. I shivered, as the air cooled around me in his absence.

"Yes, that would be ideal." I cleared my throat, trying to regain my train of thought. It was amazing how easily he derailed it. "Would it also be possible to extend one day, such as Thursday? I have a standing night out with girlfriends and I'd like to not have to juggle you and a babysitter."

"Sure, not a problem. Let me just make a note of that here," Cee said, scribbling some details onto a piece of paper. "Now, Saturday and Sundays, I usually like to have for myself, and it will let you have time with Ben as well."

"Yeah, that's fine," I nodded. As much as I would have liked it, I couldn't have him here all the time.

We continued to hash through the details, what meals he would cook, what chores he was able to do while I was away. We even broke it down to types of food Ben could have and how much TV time. I felt like I'd just discussed more than I thought was humanly possible about one job, especially a job centering on my easy-going Ben. It was more than Ben's father had ever done on the subject.

"Thank you so much for taking the time to talk with me. I know it's a tedious subject, but it helps me do a better job," Cee said as he stacked the papers. "I'll make a copy for you, and then if you think of anything, please feel free to let me know."

He stood up from the table and stretched his shoulders, raising his arms overhead, his shirt rising and revealing a sliver of his abdomen. All I could see was tight muscles and smooth skin. I shuddered, feeling the heat of desire warm me. *Why am I driving myself crazy over him? He's my nanny,* I thought to myself. *You can't have him.*

I stood up as well, glancing at the microwave so I would stop looking at him. It was already nine o'clock. I couldn't believe it took us an hour to get through all of his paper-work, but somehow, I had enjoyed every minute of it.

"I'll see you in the morning," he said quietly, putting a hand on my shoulder. I froze, not wanting him to lift it. I wanted him to touch me so much more it wasn't fair. But he was just being polite. "Most days I won't be here this late, but the first few days I understand it takes some time to work out a schedule." He let go of my shoulder and grabbed his keys. "Have a great evening, Ms. Hochs."

"Please call me Jes," I insisted, my voice low.

"Alright, goodnight... Jes."

I nearly melted at the way he smiled as he said my name.

Get over yourself, I scolded as I stood at the front door and waved Cee off into the night. *You're seeing things that aren't there.*

Yet, I loved the way my name sounded on his lips. The soft smile he got as he said it. The way his hand felt on my shoulder. I soon got wrapped up in thinking about how my name would sound across those lips when cried out in passion. My insides were screaming to make that fantasy come true, but my head drowned it out with worry and self-doubt. A sigh left my lips as I broke my gaze from the long-closed front door to head upstairs.

Ben had fallen asleep with a sports magazine across his chest, and his light still on. I picked up the magazine and put it on his nightstand. He mumbled something in his sleep, frowning at his dreams. I kissed his blond hair and slowly combed it with my fingers. With a soft smile, I turned off the light and went to my own bed. After washing my face and getting in my PJs, I lay in bed still thinking about the day. My thoughts slowly drifted to Cee.

I had promised myself that I wouldn't be interested in men, for Ben's sake. I didn't want to confuse him, and I still hurt so much from the cheating and the divorce. I turned over, fluffing the pillow and trying to get comfortable, but not succeeding. I was being stupid, and I didn't like Cee. He was just paid to hang around me, anyway.

Also, he was too young to be interested in a woman my age. Especially one with a kid. I was just attracted to him because of his great cooking, his amazing personality, his wonderful arms, his captivating eyes and his cute behind. I sighed. It had been far too long since I had any alone time with a man.

I was too hot, then too cold. I threw the covers off, then snuggled tightly in them. I knew what I needed, even though I hadn't needed it in a long time.

I no longer kept my vibrator in the drawer by my bed, not since Ben had started poking around the house. I went to my closet and reached up to the top shelf for the shoebox. I quickly turned it on to test it and nothing happened. My heart sank, until I remembered that I had taken the batteries out so that they wouldn't discharge. I found them in the shoebox and put them in. A satisfying buzz came from it as I jumped back in my bed.

My mind went to Cee, wrapping me up in torrid dreams and fantasies that I knew could never see the light of day.

"Jes," he says in a husky voice. "I have been thinking about you ever sense I saw you."

He slowly extends his hand and caresses my check, taking the back of my neck into his palm and pulling me into a passionate kiss. My hands trail up his strong arms and into his hair. I entwine my fingers in it, pulling at it slightly. He pushes further into the kiss, and spreads my lips open with his. His tongue darts in my mouth. He tastes sweet and familiar. I let out a slight moan, enjoying it as his hands pulled me in tighter, matching his tongue's motions.

Suddenly, his tongue is elsewhere. He's an eager lover, energetic with youth. I can tell that he's really enjoying it, rather than just doing it for me. I can feel his muscular arms wrapped around my legs, drawing me closer to him. I want it. I want it so bad.

50

As my vibrator pushed me to orgasm, I made sure to keep my voice down as I whimpered Cee's name. I didn't stop at just one orgasm either. I needed release after the sexual tension that I had felt today.

As I finished, I put the vibrator back in my drawer. I'd put it away tomorrow, but right now I was exhausted. Exhausted from Cee's sexual prowess. I smiled, knowing it was just a fantasy, but for now, I didn't care.

CHAPTER 8

The next few days went without any hiccups. Cee would show up in the mornings, right as I was about to head out the door. I would come home at night and Cee would tell me if anything happened that day, and let me know what was in the oven or what to do to make the dinner. He would be out the door ten minutes later, and Ben and I would spend the night talking about his day or what he learned from Cee. I always stared at him as he left, enjoying the view and wishing he would stay.

Thursday came around, and to be honest, I was excited to spend a night gossiping with the girls. They were all going to be so jealous. I came home from work to find Cee and Ben on his Xbox, playing some sort of football game.

"Who's winning?" I asked.

"I am," Ben said boastfully.

"I don't know how he's doing it," Cee said with a chuckle, and then winked at me. I couldn't help but grin back at him. He was so good with Ben.

"Don't let me interrupt. I'm just going to run upstairs and change real quick."

I shook my head as I walked upstairs and started picking out an outfit. I wanted something that would look good as I walked out the door. Something that would make Cee turn his head, and maybe even let Ben win the game for real.

I put on one of my short sundresses and twirled in the mirror. The reflection in the mirror looked good, until I saw the legs. There was dark stubble on them. I rubbed my hand up my leg and felt like sandpaper. Not shaving had finally caught up with me.

Unfortunately, I didn't have time to shave, so I grabbed my go-to maxi dress, which was dark blue with a very flattering halter top, and my chunky sandals. I snatched a bracelet to complete the outfit and was trying to work the clasp, but just couldn't get it. Who decided that clasps on bracelets were a smart idea?

"Hey, Ben," I called, coming down the stairs. "Can you help me with my bracelet? It's the one that always gets stuck."

"Hold on, Mom, please? I'm about to score," Ben called back, staring straight into the T.V. I sighed, knowing it would be a while before he even remembered to blink, let alone help me.

"Here, let me help you, Jes." Cee turned around and held out his hand. I dropped the bracelet into his palm. Holding out my arm, I tried not to look into his handsome dark violet eyes, afraid my own eyes would betray my feelings. He took the bracelet and gently wrapped it around my wrist, careful not to pinch the delicate skin. The warmth of his skin flooded my senses, and I knew I had to stop thinking what I was thinking.

But I couldn't.

His finger caressed the inside of my wrist as he latched the clasp. My mind imagined those fingers tracing up my leg inch by inch. He turned my wrist over in his hands to look at his work.

Oh my gosh, why is my face so hot? He just put on a bracelet. I shouldn't be reacting this way! I flushed with embarrassment, but he just looked up at me and smiled.

"Pretty," he said. His eyes bored through me, and for a moment I wasn't sure if he was talking about me or the bracelet. His fingers lingered against my skin, and I forgot to breathe. Tension flowed between us like electrified water, and the only sound I registered was the pounding of my own heart.

But, then, as if he thought better of it, Cee pulled his hand away from mine. The moment was gone, and he turned back around to watch Ben play the video game as if nothing had happened.

I shook myself, trying to make my body move after his touch and not quite succeeding at first. *It's all in your head,* I told myself. *Get it together. Yes, he's hot and great with your son. But he's not interested, so stop pretending like he is.* Finally, I grabbed my purse and opened the door.

"You guys have fun. I'll be back in a few hours."

"Have a great time," Cee replied, turning around to look at me. "You look amazing."

I grinned, floating on his praise. Sure, he was probably just telling the person who signed his paycheck something nice so she would keep writing those checks, but I didn't care. He thought I looked "amazing."

"Thank you, Cee," I said, not realizing how much my voice gave away of how I felt. "Bye, Ben."

Ben made a noncommittal noise, his attention firmly on the game. Cee shrugged, and smiled at me before slowly taking those beautiful eyes away and looking back at the TV.

Without his gaze on me, I suddenly remembered that I needed to breathe. I opened the front door, thankful for the calm breeze that cooled me down. I didn't know why his touch made me so bothered. Well, actually, I did. I just wasn't willing to admit it yet.

I walked to my car, absent-mindedly rubbing my wrist and thinking of Cee's hands on my skin, the way he looked at me. I quickly tried to dismiss it from my memory. It was clear that he wasn't interested in me anymore than a rock was.

Get a hold of yourself, I scolded myself silently and headed to the local bar us girls liked to escape to. *He's so out of your league, you aren't even playing the same sport.*

CHAPTER 9

I was the first to the bar, so I sat down in our normal booth and asked for a glass of wine. I ordered a Moscato, hoping that the sweet treat would take my mind off of Cee. Even as the waiter set down my glass, I was still rubbing my wrist and thinking of how his touch felt.

I took a sip, hoping that the wine would blur my thoughts so I didn't have to concentrate on how my nanny's touch was making my heart race. The wine was sweet and rich. Just the right thing to take the edge off.

It wasn't long until the all the girls arrived. Melissa arrived first, her dark hair pulled back into a slick ponytail and looking like she just stepped out of a magazine. I had been hoping Cindy would be first, but I still smiled and waved her over. She was always so perfect: perfect hair, perfect clothes, perfect men. I always felt like I was falling behind around her, even though she swore up and down I wasn't.

"Margarita, a glass of red wine, and a Manhattan," Melissa told the waiter with a smile as she slid into the booth across from me. I raised my eyebrows at the rather intense drink order. She fixed the collar on her shirt and grinned at me. "I saw Cindy and Tricia in the parking lot."

"That's good," I replied with a grin. "Otherwise I was going to ask if I had to drive you home."

Melissa laughed as Cindy walked over and sat down.

"Do I have paint in my hair again?" Cindy asked, her hand going up and checking. I shook my head at her, feeling an intense kinship. I loved my three friends, but since Cindy was the only other one with kids, I felt the closest to her.

"Just a dab of purple," Tricia teased, taking her seat. "It looks great."

Cindy rolled her eyes, knowing that we were just playing with her. The waiter carefully placed all the drinks in front of us before scampering off.

"So, Jes, how is the new nanny working out?" Cindy asked, taking a sip of her red wine and relaxing back into her seat.

I sat up a little straighter, finally feeling like I was on top of the world. I'd been waiting all week to tell them just how good Cee was.

"He is *AMAZING*. I can't believe how quickly Ben has taken to him. He cooks and cleans for me, and keeps Ben so active that each night he falls asleep almost instantly," I gushed. I could feel my cheeks heating with a happy flush.

"Wait, your nanny is a man?" Melissa asked, choking slightly on her margarita.

"Yes, I guess I forgot to mention that." I smiled and shrugged like it was nothing. Secretly though, I was loving it. Recently, all the discussion around me was about my divorce and struggle. This was the first time in months I was excited and happy. Cee was the cause of so much joy in my life.

"That is a pretty big detail to omit," Melissa said. "And, follow up question: is he cute?"

I laughed and reddened slightly. "I mean, he's not bad

looking, but he is younger than me, and you all know I've sworn off men. Especially after the way my last relationship ended." I took a big gulp of wine. I needed to convince them as much as I needed to convince myself. "Besides, I have no idea what I would do with all those muscles."

Every single one of us started to giggle.

"We may have to come over and take a look for ourselves." Melissa said, raising her margarita up in a cheers. "You know I love a good looking man."

"Tricia, what about you, how is your job going?" I asked, quickly trying to get the attention directed away from me. The thought of Cee with Melissa made me distinctly uncomfortable. I didn't want to think about what the jealous thought meant, but I knew that I didn't want Melissa within ten feet of him.

"It's going okay..." Tricia trailed off. She smiled, but the lack of light in her eyes betrayed her. "Things have been super crazy, actually. I think I might need to hire an assistant." She took a big gulp of her drink. We never understood how she did her job without one, but this was clearly a big deal to her.

"You should get one. Then, maybe you can finally take a vacation," Cindy said encouragingly. She leaned forward, her eyes taking in Tricia's exhausted appearance as only a mother could. "You work too hard. You're going to stress yourself out and get sick."

"Oh that would be nice. It's just... it's something I've always wanted to do on my own, you know? I built this company, and I just don't know if anyone can run it as well as I can." Tricia took a big sip of her Manhattan and then turned to Cindy, changing the subject as quickly as I had. "What about you, Cindy? How is your daughter doing in school now?"

Cindy started beaming. "Fantastic, she got her grades up

just in time for the beginning of her senior year. I couldn't believe it. She even got her scholarship back. That tutor we hired, Dane, was such a good influence on her. I don't even mind that they're dating now."

We all chuckled at her final statement. She had flown off the handle when she first learned of it, not wanting her daughter to be with an older man. If you could count three years as older. To hear Cindy pretend like it was no big deal, after hearing her angst over it for weeks, was worth a laugh.

"That is so great to hear!" I congratulated her. "I guess that just leaves you, Melissa. How's the last week treated you?"

"Well, you all remember that lawyer that I dated for a few weeks?" We all nodded our heads yes. How could we forget him? He was tall, dark handsome and seemed to have stepped out of the pages of a magazine. All of our jaws dropped when we first saw him. Melissa usually dated good looking, wealthy men, but this one blew them all out of the water.

"Well, it really didn't work out. He was talking about the future, and kids. I mean we had only been together for a month." She shook her head. "I just don't know what it is about men these days. I can never find one to keep around." She paused taking a sip of her margarita. "Speaking of not being able to keep something around, do you guys know of any good gardeners? Mine quit again on me."

"Why don't you try the people we used to get our nanny and tutor? They keep supplying great referrals," Cindy said pulling out a card for Melissa.

"Sure, might as well," Melissa said, taking the card. "What's the worst that could happen? Maybe the next one will even be cute."

"Maybe even as cute as Jes's nanny," Tricia teased,

bringing the focus back to me. "I still want more details. You blush too much for you not to have something good."

"I do not!" I said as my face heated, and I played with the spot on my wrist where he touched me.

"The lady doth protest too much," Cindy quoted. "Spill."

I let out a dramatic sigh. "Nothing happened." Three sets of disbelieving eyebrows raised. "Nothing!"

"Spill," Cindy repeated. "Or we're just going to keep pestering you all night. It's only going to get worse."

I glared at each of them before giving up. "I'm serious when I say nothing has happened. Cee's the ultimate gentleman. He opens doors and pulls out chairs."

"Sounds nice," Melissa said softly.

"It is," I agreed, thinking of how just the little things – making dinner, having things ready, and being there for Ben – meant to me. "Anyway, he's very professional. There's nothing going on."

"But do you want there to be?" Tricia asked, setting her empty martini glass on the table.

I played with my wineglass. "A little. But he's younger than me. He's so much better looking, and I've got a kid to think about. It just... it would never work."

"You won't know until you try," Cindy said quietly. "You never know."

"No..." I shook my head, thinking of how screwed up my life was. "I couldn't do that to him. Right now, he's my son's nanny. He's a great addition to our house, but he's not family. Besides, I need to stay away from men. And the last person I should even think about naked is my employee."

"Okay. If that's what you want," Cindy said, sitting back in her chair, her mouth disappointed.

I looked around and watched all three of my friends shrug as if I was making a mistake. But I knew I wasn't. Cee was young and wonderful, but I needed more than I could ever ask of him. He was my employee and I needed to remember that.

No matter how good he looked in his shorts.

~

I made it home to find Ben asleep on the couch, and Cee sitting next to him, reading a book. I paused for a moment, enjoying the domestic tranquility of the scene. It felt so right that my heart ached for something I knew I could never have. Cee was our nanny. He had to leave at the end of the night.

"Have fun?" I whispered to Cee, quietly placing my purse on the kitchen table.

"Yeah, we watched a movie and had some pizza. He crashed a little bit ago, and I've just been reading this book." He held it up. It was a romance book I kept on the table. "Interesting reading material you keep around the house." He was joking, and maybe a little sarcastic, but it was cute.

I blushed. I kept it there because I thought the cover was pretty and I almost never had anyone over.

"It's just a romance novel. And I like the cover," I admitted shyly. I would never tell him that I actually enjoyed the racy story.

"It's quite steamy," he joked, wiggling his eyebrows and making his violet eyes sparkle. "It's giving me all kinds of interesting ideas."

I coughed, trying to avoid eye contact with him. Cee and steamy were the two words I was trying to keep separate in my head.

"Thank you so much for staying late tonight. It's nice to get out with the girls," I replied quickly, trying to change the subject back to something more appropriate for a working relationship. I looked at Ben, still soundly asleep on the couch. "Let me get him in bed, and then I can write you a check."

I walked over to Ben to lift him up and wondered how he had gotten so much bigger the past few days. He barely fit in my arms, and I had to use all my strength just to lift him from the couch. A pang in my heart reminded me that Ben wouldn't always be little.

"I got him, Jes." Cee stood up and took Ben from me with ease. The young boy cuddled into Cee's shoulder and gripped him tight. I walked behind as Cee carried Ben up the stairs.

I was very thankful to be behind him, as I got to watch Cee's ass in front of me. I wondered just how much I had been drinking to stare so openly, especially since he was holding my son in his arms.

We made it to Ben's room and got him all tucked in. He smiled in his sleep, his lips curling up into what I imagined was the reaction of a good dream. I bent over to give him a kiss goodnight, and tucked the sheets around his arms. He was getting so big. One day he wouldn't let me do this anymore. No matter what, it would be too soon.

We tiptoed out of the room, turning off the light as Cee closed the door behind me. A stray shoe left in the hallway tripped me up and I almost took a tumble. Cee reached out and caught me. He felt so warm against my body, his strong arms wrapped around me.

I flushed unexpectedly, unsure if it was the alcohol or the fact that I had enjoyed the moment of warmth from another person. It had been a long time since anyone had touched me. *Breathe,* I reminded myself.

As cliché as it sounded, he'd taken my breath away.

Before I could embarrass myself further, I hurried back down the stairs, hoping that he didn't see my red cheeks. Once I was in the living room, I busied myself with looking for the checkbook.

Play it cool, Jes. Remember what you said to the girls. You aren't ready for a relationship and even if you were, the nanny is not the appropriate person to have one with.

"Thanks again, Cee. I really do appreciate it. I'll see you tomorrow." I smiled, finally looking up at him through my eyelashes as I handed him the check. I was scared that if I looked at him directly that I would start to blush again.

Cee took the check, carefully folding it into his back pocket as I looked for something else to keep my hands busy. I played with the bracelet, suddenly hoping he'd help me take it off.

Stop it. You can't have him.

"Sure thing. Ben is really a great kid." He reached for the door. His hand hesitated at the handle, his face turned towards me. His violet eyes were warm and held me captive. "It's really great to see you having a good time. I'm glad I got to see that beautiful smile of yours."

I blinked. Did he really just say that?

Before I could ask him, he opened the door. With one hand on the doorknob, he reached over and touched my shoulder. I trembled slightly. "I'll see you in the morning," he said. "Hope to see you smiling."

I tried to respond but my mouth couldn't form the words of a simple goodbye. This wasn't a dream. He actually said those words.

He thought my smile was beautiful. No one had ever told me they thought my smile was beautiful.

The door made a quiet click as I closed and locked it. I couldn't believe he made me so flustered. Yet, even though I wasn't really ready to admit it to myself, I had rather enjoyed it.

What was I thinking? He was my nanny. He was younger than me.

But he thought my smile was beautiful.

CHAPTER 10

Cee held me against his smooth chest, those eyes blazing as he dipped down to kiss my jawbone, then on towards my neck. Each small kiss made me moan just a little louder...

Instead of moaning, however, I heard the beeping of my alarm clock as it pulled me out of the dream. I groaned and wished I could ignore it for another few hours. I wanted to finish the dream, to let him take me all the way to the edge.

My dreams were the only place where I knew I could have Cee and not feel any guilt about who he was or what his age was. Dreams were where anything was possible. There was no judgment in dreams, just release. My muscles protested as I stretched and tried to get the motivation to put my feet on the floor.

I heard Cee's car pull up just as I was putting the final touches on my wardrobe. My traitorous heart fluttered at the sound. I checked myself in the mirror and frowned when I saw the woman staring back at me. She looked tired. And frumpy.

I stretched out the cardigan over the bulge in my jeans and hoped the wear would give a bit more as the day went on. I refused to go up a size and I had nothing else clean. I thought of changing, but the only other wearable thing in my closet was a cocktail dress, and that wasn't going to work either.

"Morning, Cee," I said as I stepped into the kitchen, where Cee and Ben were engaged in conversation at the kitchen table. I smiled and rummaged in the pantry, grabbing a couple PowerBars. *Breakfast of champions,* I thought. "What are you guys planning to do today?"

"I think we're going to go to the beach. Maybe do some swimming and training for lacrosse. Nothing says fun quite like running on a beach." He smiled at Ben before handing me my travel mug full of coffee. Our fingertips touched and sent an electric tingle up my arm. His touch jolted me awake better than any cup of coffee could.

"Sounds entertaining. Let me know if you need anything from me. Hopefully I'll be home early." I took the cup from him and gave Ben a quick kiss on the head, trying to disguise the blush heating my cheeks. How in the world was I going to survive an entire summer of this?

The day seemed to never end. I watched the clock slowly tick by. Wednesdays were normally the busiest day. I was having a hard time concentrating on my computer screen, as my mind drifted to Cee's comment about seeing me happy. The way he looked at me, just for a split second, it seemed like he was interested.

In me. Frumpy, bumpy, divorcee me.

I laughed at my own craziness. I was imagining things.

Finally, 4:30 decided to show up. I hastily grabbed my

purse and headed out the door. I arrived back home to the boys playing out in the yard, passing a ball back and forth with the lacrosse sticks, laughing and talking.

It was what I always wanted for Ben. What his dad never even cared to try. A boy playing catch in the yard. Ben was happy and that was all that should matter.

I watched for a moment, enjoying seeing my son smile. Not only that, I enjoyed watching Cee's muscular form move around the yard. My breath caught in my throat, as I stared at Cee. He had taken his shirt off, the heat of the day pounding down on him until those chiseled muscles gleamed with perspiration.

It was the kind of thing that I happily committed to memory so that I could hopefully have it appear in my dreams tonight, because that was the only way I was ever going to see those muscles again.

I got out of the car and ambled up to the house, focusing on each step I took. *He is our nanny. He is too young for me*, I kept repeating in my head. There were a million reasons why the two of us would never work out and I needed to stop my silly crush before I let it turn into anything else.

Ben waved at me and I focused all my attention on him. Otherwise, the drool would start to escape my lips.

"Hi, Mom. Were almost done here. Just a few more minutes if that's okay," Ben pleaded.

How about a few more years? That may be enough time for me to truly appreciate this Greek god in front of me.

"Sure, as long as we don't hold Cee up," I answered. I felt my vocal cords constrict. All of my blood was leaving my head and heading down south with each flex of his arms. It was not fair that the man looked that good. It was impossible not to look.

"Nah, I'm all good. I don't have plans till later." Cee yelled, easily tossing the ball back to Ben. It flew past his shoulder and down into the bushes. With a groan of annoyance, Ben turned and chased it down the lawn. I tried to hold back a grin, glad to have Cee around for even a few more moments.

I sat down on the front porch to watch the two of them play. Glancing at the neighbor's windows, I had a feeling I wasn't the only lonely housewife watching Cee work out. It was too good to pass up.

I rolled up my pants and absorbed the warm rays from the sun. I closed my eyes, letting my thoughts drift. *What if,* floated through my mind. The thought of having a man who was not only sexy as hell, but also cared about my son, was a fantasy I could happily stay in. It was a daydream that went on and on until cruelly interrupted by a horrible buzzing noise.

Damn it. I looked around, not recognizing the sound, and then found a phone sitting on the porch.

"Hey Cee, I think your phone is ringing?" I yelled, holding it up at him.

"Who's calling?" Cee yelled back.

"It looks like a... Grace?" I said, suddenly realizing what the name meant. Of course he would have a girlfriend, how could he not? I bit the inside of my cheek, scolding myself for getting carried away with someone who was obviously taken. It was silly of me to even let myself pretend that he was single. The man could cook and was good with kids; there was no way he was still on the market.

"Oh?" He stopped throwing the ball and sprinted over. I tossed him his phone.

"Hey, is everything okay?" he said into the phone as he turned and walked away. "Okay, yeah, good to know. Well, will tonight still be good?" He paused, kicking his feet back and forth over the grass. Ben made his way to me.

"Who's he talking to, Mom?" Ben asked.

"I'm not sure, but it doesn't really matter. You know, Cee

does have a life outside of us," I joked, nudging him in the ribs. Ben just rolled his eyes at me.

"Perfect, thanks for letting me know and I'll be there. Can't wait." He smiled as he hung up and strolled back to us.

"Who was that?" Ben asked.

"Ben, you know it's none of our business," I scolded, but I was secretly glad my child had asked the question that was burning me from the inside.

"It was just a friend with a slight change in plans tonight." *Just a friend,* I thought with relief. *Not a girlfriend.*

"Ben, I have to go and get changed." Cee grabbed his shirt from the lawn. "I hope you had fun today. Make sure to tell your mom all about it." He turned toward me, his eyes bright and his young face eager. "Have a good evening, Jes."

He offered his hand to help pull me up from my sitting position. I happily took it and enjoyed the warm sensation that crept up my arm as he pulled me up. I was not expecting to be pulled up so quickly, and I fell forward with momentum. In my stumble, I extended my other hand, landing on his chest in an attempt to steady myself. I immediately blushed as I felt the hard muscle underneath it.

"Thanks," I gasped, my heart pounding out of control.

"I'll see you tomorrow," Cee whispered. He was so close to me I could feel the electricity between us. He eyes seemed to be darker than normal, but with a blink of his eye they returned to their violet color. My hand gave a slight wave as he pulled away and put on his shirt. I was actually disappointed that I wouldn't get to see him for a few hours.

I'm just going to miss my eye candy, I told myself. *That's all. That's all this is.*

I was a big, fat liar and I knew it.

CHAPTER 11

he next morning, I woke up before the alarm for the first time in weeks, determined to look nice for Cee for a change. Maybe I'd even curl my hair.

Yeah, right, I told myself, glancing at the clock. I would be lucky to put on earrings at my current pace. Just because I was up and motivated, didn't mean I was actually getting anything done.

I pulled out a long dark skirt and a flowery blouse that I always thought accentuated my figure. It played to my strengths, the few of them I felt like I still had. The shirt gave just a hint of cleavage and the skirt made my ass look like a million bucks.

It was silly, but I couldn't help it. I wanted to look like a million bucks. I wanted Cee to look at me like a million bucks.

I paused in the mirror, thinking. Why was I doing this? He was our nanny. He was younger than me. He had shown almost no interest in me. So he thought I had a beautiful smile, so what? That could be platonic.

But I didn't want it to be.

68

I closed my eyes and pressed my fingers into my scalp. Why did I want him to care so much? I shouldn't and I knew it. But that didn't change the flutter in my stomach at the thought of him seeing me this morning and telling me I looked nice.

I put the finishing touches on my makeup, wishing I had a few more hours to perfect my look, as I heard his car pull into the driveway. I stepped back. This was as good as it was going to get.

I hurried downstairs to let him in, smiling brightly as I opened the door to let him in.

"Wow," Cee remarked, taking a step back. "You look great. Big meeting today?"

"Thanks." I flushed with pleasure, loving the way his eyes traveled up and down my body. For the first time in months, I felt at least slightly attractive. I knew that my muffin top was bulging slightly and that the shirt was a little tight across my shoulders, but when Cee said I looked nice, I believed him.

"I, uh..." Cee shook his head as if I was distracting him. The thought made me laugh and preen just a little. "I got you some coffee on my way. I was stopping and thought you would like some and..."

He trailed off, then handed me the coffee before stepping into the house. Compliments and gifts from a sexy guy. This day was already shaping up to be the best Monday in the history of ever.

"Ben's still sleeping," I told him, closing the door behind him. "He wanted to stay up and watch this old dinosaur movie with me. I figured he didn't have school today, so..."

I trailed off, suddenly worried that I might have upset Cee's plans with Ben.

"That's fine." Cee grinned. "I used to love it whenever my mom let me stay up late. Besides, you and Ben come first."

"Oh." I was struck at how different Cee and my ex-husband were. Richard would have berated me. Even if he didn't have plans with Ben, Richard would have made a big deal about how I had upset him. It was a welcome change to have someone trust my judgment about my son.

"Do you want some breakfast?" Cee asked, rubbing the stubble on his chin. "I mean, for you and Ben?"

"That would be great," I stammered, suddenly nervous. It was just breakfast. Cee made breakfast for us everyday. I had no reason to suddenly be nervous about being alone with Cee. But we usually had Ben as a buffer.

"What would you like? French toast? Pancakes?" Cee asked. He moved through the kitchen, pulling out pans and bowls. He looked so comfortable there. So right.

"Pancakes would be great," I answered. "Can I help?"

"Sure." Cee grinned at me. "If you'll grab the eggs and the milk, I'll start mixing everything together."

I went to the fridge and pulled out the eggs and a gallon of milk, turning slowly to watch Cee as he rummaged in the pantry for the flour and sugar. He moved so smoothly that it was intoxicating to watch him. He turned and caught my gaze, and I quickly turned bright red at being caught.

"Here," I offered, putting the milk on the counter as if I hadn't just been staring at him.

"Thanks," he murmured, grinning at my obvious red face. "Will you grab the spatula? It should be in the drawer over there."

I turned to the drawer, searching for the plastic spatula that I knew he preferred. The idea that I knew which of my spatulas he preferred made me pause. It was so comfortable to have him here. So right. A tightness, a longing that I couldn't control was growing in my chest.

"I found it," I announced, turning around just as Cee

stepped back with the bowl full of batter. We collided, and the batter went flying into the air.

I watched as the bowl fell in slow motion and splattered all over my dress.

"Oh, Jes, I'm so sorry." Cee stared at my ruined outfit. Not even the top had been spared. He grabbed a towel from the counter and tried to brush some of the batter from my shoulder. So much for my hot outfit.

"It's fine," I said, catching his hand in mine. He was so warm and strong beneath my fingers. And close. For the briefest moment, I considered kissing him. It felt like I could, like this could be our moment.

He reached toward my face and my breath hitched in my lungs. His violet eyes locked on mine and I forgot how to breathe. His strong hands caressed my cheek and I nearly melted into a puddle of desire. "You have batter on your face."

"Oh," I whimpered, hating the way my voice came out heated and full of desire. I cleared my throat. His fingers stroked my cheek and it took all that I had not to lean into him and beg for more.

There was a small sound behind me, and he pulled away as if burned by my touch.

"Mom?" Ben's voice filled the kitchen and I knew why Cee had stepped back. "What happened?"

"We had a little accident," Cee informed him, his voice deeper and richer than I remembered. "So, now we're having French toast. Will you go grab the bread from the counter, please?"

"Sure." Ben looked at me for a moment. "You can't wear that to work, Mom."

"Thanks." I said, trying not to roll my eyes. "I'll go change."

"I'll have breakfast done when you come back down," Cee promised.

"I'll be right back."

I darted upstairs, desperate not to have the heat of desire flowing through me. He had touched me. *Caressed* me. It was making my heart do funny things and my stomach was performing flip-flops.

I quickly changed into a pair of slacks and a light v-neck shirt. It wasn't anything as nice as my previous outfit, but at least it wasn't jeans and a t-shirt either. I checked the mirror to find my eyes shining and my cheeks flushed. I barely looked like myself. I looked like I was ready for sex.

It was a look that was not appropriate for my six-year-old son and his nanny. I splashed cold water onto my face, unable to get the excitement off my face. I would just have to deal with it, since now I was running late.

I hurried down the stairs, hearing Ben laugh at Cee's retelling of the pancake accident. I smiled and ducked my head into the kitchen.

"Pancake lady has to get to work," I interrupted. "You be good today, Ben. I have my girl's night out tonight, so I'll come up and tuck you in when I get home tonight."

"Have a good day at work, Mom," Ben replied, smiling at me from his big plate of French toast.

My stomach grumbled, but I needed to get going. I gave them both a wave and hurried to the front door.

"Wait," Cee called out after me. "Here, have some break-fast, and don't forget your coffee."

I turned at the doorway and he handed me my cup of coffee and a napkin-wrapped sandwich of French toast and eggs. He must have made the sandwich just for me, knowing I was going to be running late. I couldn't wipe the grin of my face.

"Thank you," I said softly, completely taken aback at the

simple yet sweet thought. I didn't think, I just moved forward, meaning to kiss his cheek.

Unfortunately, he turned into it and I kissed his lips. His soft, perfect, warm lips. I reacted like I'd touched lightning.

"Oh, I'm so sorry," I gasped, taking a step back and wishing I had a spare hand to press to my mortified face. Instead, I focused on not dropping my sandwich or coffee. "I didn't mean to do that."

Cee blinked twice. "My fault. I turned my head. Don't worry about it." He smiled, his eyes dark and absorbing me. "You should go or you're going to be late."

"Right." I didn't move. "Again, I'm so sorry..."

"I moved into it. Nothing happened." He gave me a gentle push on the back of my shoulder. "Go to work and have a good time out tonight. I'll see you when you get home."

"Okay," I whispered, turning and heading out the door. I nearly turned around to apologize again, but I knew it wouldn't do anything. Hopefully, he just thought I was a disorganized mess and never brought it up again.

I set the coffee and sandwich down in the car, finally pressing a hand to my swollen lips. He had felt so good. His lips had felt so good pressed to mine. Even though it was an accidental kiss, I wished I could have another.

He's the nanny, I reminded myself. But today, that didn't seem like much of an obstacle. Especially because he hadn't drawn back from the kiss either.

What was I thinking? There was no way I could do this.

CHAPTER 12

I didn't mention the kiss to the girls at Girl's Night. I didn't want them analyzing it and telling me it really was just an accident, and that I shouldn't be reading anything into it. I wanted to keep it for myself for a bit, so instead I simply kept quiet and said that Cee was still amazing for Ben.

I came home from the girls' night out to find my ex-husband's car in the driveway.

Oh no, I immediately thought. My stomach dropped, anxiety overwhelming me. I never told Richard about Cee. I had mentioned a nanny, but never a male nanny. And I definitely hadn't said that he would be staying late tonight.

Ever the controlling force, he would be seething if he felt like I kept something from him. I shouldn't have cared. I mean, after all, he did keep his mistress from me, but old habits took over as I imagined the fallout.

I leaped out of my car and darted up the lawn. I could just make out the outlines of Richard and Cee standing on the doorstep, illuminated by the dim porch light. Richard's wiry frame only came up to Cee's chin, and his belly protruded slightly over his black tailored suit pants.

To be fair, he was in prime physical condition when we married. Years of office work had taken its toll. He had neglected his body just as he had neglected me. All he had ever cared about was staying longer at the office than anyone else, even if it meant that he missed going to the gym or eating dinner with his wife and son.

"Who are you to think you have the right to take care of my son? I don't know you. I have no idea who you are." Richard's voice was carrying across the yard, rising in pitch and anger. He held up his expensive phone and waved it under Cee's nose. "I just got this text from my son saying that he and a 'C'" have been practicing and I should come to his game."

"Sir, I tried to let you know who I am. I'm the nanny who's been hired on. I've been here for almost a month. We can call Jes again if you don't believe me," Cee interrupted politely, somehow maintaining a calm voice.

"I tried calling Jes, but she ignored me," Richard yelled. I hated the way he twisted my name into something akin to a swear word. "I drive all the way over here to see her gone and you sitting there watching TV. You won't even let me in to my own house to see my son!" Richard screeched, pushing Cee in the chest with his index finger. His glasses teetered on the edge of his nose, threatening to fall off thanks to the waterfall of sweat pouring down him now.

"Richard!" I called as I made it up to the door. "Hi, I am so sorry. I completely forgot to tell you about the new nanny." I don't know why I apologized; I didn't need to. Sole custody meant that all of my choices were my own. Still, I persisted. "This is Stacey, and he has been watching out for Ben for the past few weeks."

I smiled as sweetly as possible, hoping to keep Richard from starting a fight. I knew it wasn't going to be enough, so I pushed my way in between the two men. My heart pounded in my chest as I considered the possible outcomes. None of them were pretty. Being shorter than average, Richard always had a point to make with bigger guys. He wasn't about to back down.

My eyes darted to Cee, who was a statue. His jaw was clenched so hard a vein pounded just beneath the surface, visible to all. Those dark violet eyes stared at the little man, and I wondered what he was thinking.

"You *FORGOT* to tell me?" Richard turned his anger toward me and got in my face. "He's my son! I should be kept informed if some strange man is watching out for him. He could be a criminal for all we know."

The sweat from his face flew onto mine as he bobbed his head at each word to punctuate it. I wiped the beads from my forehead, disgusted. My voice had left me and I was unable to come up with a response. He was always able to turn it back on me and make me believe it was my fault.

I shrank, unable to find the words to defend myself, let alone Cee.

"Excuse me, Richard?" Cee said in a flat tone. He stepped in front of me so that he could face Richard directly, blocking me from Richard's wrath. I could tell Cee was trying to control his temper. His hands were clenched in a tight fists and every move he made screamed with carefully controlled fury.

"I'm sorry that I didn't know who you were. I've been working with Ben for almost a month now. I've never seen you at any of his games, or heard about any quality time you spent with him. Ben talks about you like you moved to another country."

Richard's mouth opened to continue on his tirade, but Cee cut him off before he even started.

"Stop right there. Maybe if you were involved in Ben's life a bit more, you would have met me sooner." Cee's voice didn't get louder, but he was getting angrier with each word. It was like we were in the eye of the storm; it seemed calm, but you knew that any second something would change.

"I'm involved in my son's life just fine, thank you very much. I'm his father!" Richard waved a fist under Cee's nose. Cee stood motionless against the threat. He took a big breath in, making his chest puff out farther.

"When was the last time you went to one of his games? When's the last time you sat down with your son and talked to him?" Cee asked quietly. It was only because I had been observing him so closely that I knew he was angry. Otherwise, he looked completely calm.

"How dare you!" Richard spat. He stepped up closer to Cee.

"You're so lucky that you have such an amazing kid. You never know when someone you love will be taken away." Cee tucked his chin and looked Richard in the eye. He was so close he was fogging up Richard's glasses with each breath. "I can tell that you think you have all the time in the world, but one day they are just gone. A part of you is just gone. Don't deny him the bond that only a parent can share with his child."

"You have no right to talk to me this way!" Richard hollered, spit flying as the words came out. A few beads landed on Cee, but he didn't seem to even notice. Richard pushed Cee's chest with his finger, trying to get Cee to react. To fight him. My ex-husband wasn't the kind of person who took criticism well, especially from a more masculine man like Cee.

When Cee just stood there, taking it without reacting, Richard turned on me. "Are you going to let the help talk to me this way?"

I grimaced, not knowing how to respond. I never did know how to respond when Richard got like this. I opened my mouth to reply and Cee put a hand gently on my shoulder. Suddenly, I found my inner strength.

"Yes, I am. He's right. He's finally put into words everything that I have been thinking about for the past few months. You should listen to his advice." I felt liberated as the words left my mouth. I had wanted to tell Richard this, and never had the courage, but Cee had helped me express it. "You're missing out on the best part of Ben's life."

Richard's mouth fell open like a fish gulping for air. His face started to turn a deep shade of crimson. I don't think I had ever spoke to him like that, and now that I had, he didn't know how to react. His meek, submissive nothing of an ex-wife suddenly had a little bit of a backbone.

Richard stammered and then tightened his fists, looking to continue this fight. He was a little man and needed to prove that he wasn't scared. "How dare you! You can't…"

"Daddy!" Ben opened up the front door and ran straight for Richard's arms, stopping whatever Richard had been thinking of saying. "Daddy, I missed you! I've tried texting you but you didn't answer."

Richard seemed taken off guard. He snapped out of his anger at the sight of his son. "Hi, Ben, I'm so sorry. Did we wake you up? We were just talking." His face was still red, but he bent down to give Ben a hug, looking up and glaring at me and Cee as if it were our fault.

"Have you met Cee?" Ben tugged on his father's hand to greet the other man. "He's my best friend this summer. He taught me loads of stuff about lacrosse, but I told him I want to learn about football to make you happy." Ben smiled, looking up at his father, then Cee, and then to me.

I blinked away my tears. Ben deserved someone so much better for a father. I wanted to give him so much more than that. He deserved someone who loved Ben for Ben, not for what Ben could do for him.

Richard knelt, drawing Ben to him. "You really love lacrosse, don't you?"

"Yes," Ben said slowly, never taking his eyes from his father. "But you don't. I want to make you happy. I miss you."

Richard looked up at me, and then at Cee with a frown. Understanding slowly filled his green eyes as Ben continued to talk about all of the facts he learned about football and how he was going to play the same position that Richard did.

"I don't really like it too much, but I hope I can be just as good as you were. I'll work hard and then maybe you'll come to my games," Ben said. He paused, frowning slightly and looking up at his beloved father with hope.

Realization slowly crossed Richards face, painful and harsh. It finally dawned on him that he was not a part of his son's life like he should be. This man that he had just met knew more about his son, and was also a better father figure.

"Oh, Ben, you don't have to do that. Your mom and Cee said you're great at lacrosse and really like it. It makes me happy to see you happy." His voice cracked and his color slowly returned back to normal. There it was. The reason I stayed with him for so long. When he was here, he really did care. The man wasn't pure evil, as much as I wanted him to be.

"But you don't come to my games, and you never want to hang out on the weekends. You're always hanging out with that bitch…"

"*BEN*, I told you to never say that word again," I cautioned. I cringed, knowing that he picked up that word from me. I'd said it in a moment of anger, and immediately regretted it. Well, at least regretted saying it in front of him.

Richard looked at me with disgust, and I heard Cee try to

stifle a laugh. It was rather hypocritical of Richard, considering the circumstances.

Richard faced Ben again. "I promise to come to your games every week. I'll talk to your mom and see if I can have you for a weekend, and we'll hang out the whole time. Just like we used to." Richard hugged Ben. I hoped he would keep this promise.

He looked at Ben the same way as the first day he held him, full of love and hope. It was almost enough to make me feel some remorse for my anger at him. Almost. I knew who Richard really was, and the last thing I wanted was for him to disappoint Ben again. If he let his son down for yet another time, I would have to kill him.

Ben yawned, his jaw nearly cracking from going so wide. It was way past his bedtime, and he still had a busy day in front of him tomorrow.

"Ben, I think it's time you go back to bed," Cee said softly. He made a small motion, but nothing that said he was taking Ben from Richard. With a final hug, Richard released Ben.

"Bye, Dad. Will you really come to my game this weekend?" My heart ached with the expectant hope in Ben's voice.

"Of course, Ben. I'll see you at your game," Richard replied. His voice was full of promise. I closed my eyes and sent up a silent prayer that he would actually keep this one. There were so many broken promises littered around Richard that it was difficult to believe he would keep even one as simple as coming to a game.

Cee held out his hand for Ben and together, they went inside, leaving me and Richard out on the patio. Awkward silence surrounded us as we stood there, unable to say anything to each other.

I didn't know how to spend time alone with him anymore. He wasn't the man I had married eight years ago. Hell, he wasn't even the man I knew two years ago. My skin crawled as I considered all the things he'd done to me. I finally broke and spoke first.

"I'm sorry, Richard. I forgot to tell you about the nanny. I didn't think it was a big deal," I started. Guilt flared up in my stomach. I could have prevented this entire thing with a simple voice mail message.

Richard held up his hand for me to stop. "Jes, I don't really want to hear your apology. This is not about you and me. This is about Ben." He shook his head slowly, turning to face out to the night sky. "The fact that this nanny knows more about my son then I do…it's upsetting to me."

Richard turned back to look at me, the porch light surrounding the two of us like our own little island in the dark. "I'm glad you got an extra set of hands. He seems protective of Ben. I can appreciate that, and Ben seems to like him too. But if you think I'll help pay for this Cee character, you are fucking wrong."

And there was the man I learned to despise, always about the money.

"I better get back to Ginger. She's been waiting up for me," Richard said as he walked out of the light and to his car. The mention of his other woman jogged me out of my memories.

I gave a half-hearted wave goodbye, turning out the porch light and heading inside. Closing the door, I pulled myself up the stairs. I was emotionally drained. I needed to see Ben, to know he was all right. I went into his room to see Cee tucking him in. Carefully, I went to Ben, avoiding the strewn about lacrosse sticks. He definitely needed to clean up his room tomorrow, but for tonight I just wanted to give him a kiss and tuck him in bed like I always did.

"I love you," I murmured to him as I bent over to kiss his forehead. He closed his eyes and snuggled into his pillow, already most of the way back to dreamland.

I smoothed his hair one last time before following Cee out of the bedroom. He gently shut the door behind us. I rested against the hallway wall and wiped away a tear that trickled down my cheek. I couldn't contain it any longer.

A warm arm wrapped around me, and I leaned into it. It provided a comfort that I needed so much. Tears streamed down my face, and my shoulders shook with each breath I took. The pit that had been growing in my stomach finally swallowed me whole. I could no longer hold back the pain. His arm flexed and pulled me into his chest. I buried my face in his shirt and sobbed. I felt foolish letting my emotions out like that in front of him, in front of anyone. I normally waited until I was in bed alone before I broke down.

This added comfort of having him, though, made me feel better. I wasn't forced to hold my misery in and share it with a pillow. I sobbed, letting the ache soothe itself against his strong chest.

After a few minutes with his strong arms wrapped around me, I was all cried out. I stayed against his chest, enjoying the warmth and security it gave as I sniffed and searched for the calm after the storm. I never wanted to move from his grasp. I was safe here, in his arms. It didn't hurt when I was with him.

I concentrated on the way his chest expanded with each breath he took in, his arms as they gently rubbed my back in comfort, and his breath as it tickled my cheek. I wanted to feel him move beneath me, feel his skin rub against mine and absorb his warmth like a sponge.

I wanted more. I wanted him.

I took a step back from his grasp, shocked at my own thought. I was crying a moment ago, and now I wanted sex.

No. It wasn't right. I wiped my eyes and noticed my fingers covered in mascara. *Great, I probably look as awful as I feel.*

With a big sniffle, I tried to control my runny nose and

debated what to do next. As I stood there, torn between crying and lust, a laugh escaped my lips. I was embarrassed, for the situation and from my emotions. I covered my mouth to hold in the laughter, but it didn't work. Cee looked at me confused, and cocked his head to the side.

"What's so funny?" he asked.

"Just that I don't pay you enough for this job. You're probably used to a four-year-old girl crying over a scraped knee, not a full grown woman breaking down." The laugh threatened to turn into a sob again.

"It's okay," he cooed. "At least with the four-year-old, I can give them some candy to make them happy. I don't really know how to make a grown woman feel better."

"Wine," I said with an exasperated chuckle, wiping at a fresh set of tears on my cheeks.

"Let's go get you a glass, then." His hands went to my shoulders, as his eyes evaluated me for a moment before letting me go completely. "You go sit down and I'll get it. Just relax."

I followed him down the stairs and collapsed onto the couch. I watched the particles of dust floating in the air, dancing in the rays of lamplight and the paused TV. I wanted to stay like this forever, not moving, not thinking, just watching the dust. Dust didn't have children aching for their fathers. Dust didn't have ridiculously attractive men bringing them wine who were barely old enough to drink it themselves. Dust had it easy.

"I can't find the wine. Looks like you have some whiskey, though. Would that work for you?" Cee called from the kitchen. I reluctantly left the world of dust. I couldn't have stayed there anyway.

"Sure," I called back, my voice thick and broken from crying.

Cee brought out a tumbler and a bottle of whiskey. I

watched as he poured me a couple fingers' worth. He handed me the glass.. I sipped it greedily, feeling the warmth go straight into my belly. I let out a breath that I had been holding on to for hours, and I allowed myself to relax, the muscles unclenching one by one until I was finally at ease. Cee watched me with careful eyes.

"You know what would make this better?" I asked, closing my eyes and focusing on the taste of the whiskey.

"What?"

"You having a bit too. It's so depressing to drink alone, especially after a night like this."

"Are you sure?" His voice was deep and soothing. "I try to keep business and personal life separate."

"Let me check with your boss." I looked up at the ceiling and nodded my head. "She said it was fine." I winked at him.

Cee rolled his eyes, and went to grab a glass from the kitchen. He sat back down on the couch and poured himself a small amount. It wasn't much more than a sip, but at least I didn't feel alone.

"What are you watching?" I asked as Cee took a tiny sip from his glass. The TV was on pause. There were two women yelling at each other, and two girls in ballet outfits standing near by.

"Oh, nothing," he said quickly. Too quickly. I grabbed the remote before he had a chance and hit the info button.

"Is this what I think it is?" I looked at him shocked. "You're the one who's been watching my reality show? I thought it was the TV being strange again."

He looked at me a bit ashamed. His cheeks reddened and carried the color up to his ears.

"Yes," he bashfully admitted. "I put it on because there was nothing else to watch, and then I got sucked in to it. It's like a car crash, you just can't look away."

I chuckled, reveling in the discovery. "It is kind of addicting. Especially when all the moms are fighting about what outfit their daughter should wear or how the judges screwed their kids over in scoring. I see you've almost caught up to where I am."

"I have a little bit left on this episode. Do you want to finish it with me?"

"I'd like that," I answered truthfully. "I'm not quite ready to be alone tonight, and some stupid reality TV sounds pretty good right now."

He settled into the couch a little bit more, his leg bumping up against mine. I could feel the low warmth of his body heat through my skirt. It was enough to make me hate that I didn't have on a shorter dress. I wanted to feel his skin against my own.

Shaving on a daily basis must start occurring, I thought.

"Here's to one of the weirdest nights of my life as a nanny," he cheered, lifting his glass into the air. Cee paused to look at me, and I felt like my soul was being absorbed into his intense violet eyes. I was naked underneath his gaze. Exposed. I knew he could see how tangled up and confused I was inside.

Not only about my son, but about how he made me feel as well.

As quick as that premonition came, it was gone. Instead, I was just some silly woman staring into the eyes of my babysitter.

"Cheers," I replied meekly, clinking my glass against his.

He sipped, and then frowned, looking into his glass. "I'm sorry that I didn't realize he was your ex-husband and let him into the house. I hope I didn't step out of bounds."

"No, not at all," I finally replied, glancing away from him. "Richard has a bark much bigger than his bite."

The way he was looking at me made me nervous, so to distract myself I ran my fingers through my hair to pull it up into a bun. The motion made my leg drift closer to his, and I tensed. I tried to distract myself from my leg quivering, but it was hard with him so close. My body was responding in ways my brain wasn't prepared to consider. He was the nanny, not a potential suitor. I pulled my hair hard.

"I'm glad to know you're so protective of my son, and thanks for being his best friend," I added, feeling a bit lame.

"It's my pleasure," he replied. For a moment, it seemed like he might say something more, but then instead he just nodded toward the remote. "Do you want to hit play, or do you want me to do it?"

I flashed him a smile and hit play. At least, I knew that despite it all, I didn't have to watch bad TV alone.

moaned as the incessant beeping from my phone pulled me from my heavy sleep. My eyes adjusted slowly to the morning light streaming in from the window. I focused on my brown living room table. My head was clouded with sleep and it took me a moment to realize I was on my couch. I had dozed off and never made it to my room.

After my head had finally cleared, I sat up and saw that my pillow was Cee's leg. What was worse was I had left a huge drool spot on it. My mouth dropped open. I was mortified. I really was a four-year-old girl.

I sat up as I felt Cee stirring beneath me. He'd fallen asleep sitting on the couch just like I had, his head resting on the top of the couch cushion and his arms stretched out along the back. His hair was illuminated by the morning sun, the bright red highlights like warm fire. I watched his eyelashes flutter under his mussed hair. I quickly tried to fix my own hair and wipe off the remaining drool before he fully awakened.

"Oh man, what happened?" he asked, rubbing his neck.

His voice was heavy with sleep, but in a way that made me warm.

"I think we fell asleep last night on the couch," I said as I straightened the top of my disheveled dress. I could already feel the blush threatening to overwhelm me.

"Oh wow, I'm sorry, I didn't realize I was that tired. I should have left earlier." He raised his arms above his head letting out a small grunt. "But I see you made yourself quite comfortable," he commented as he straightened out his pants, making the drool spot more noticeable.

"That's embarrassing. I'm so sorry. When I'm really tired I tend to drool a lot," I said, looking down to hide my humiliated face. He always seemed to catch me at my worst.

He chuckled. "It's okay. I'm glad I was a comfortable pillow. I wouldn't look nearly as good as you do if I'd fallen asleep on someone's lap." He stood up slowly, working out his leg muscles. I straightened up beside him and stretched out my back, hearing a pop.

He looked at his watch.

"I'm going to run home real quick and shower. I'll see you in a little bit." He reached over and gave me a hug and a quick kiss on the cheek. I was surprised how soft his lips were. It was something that I had been longing for, ever since I started having those naughty dreams. He abruptly became rigid, realizing what he just did.

"I'm sorry, I shouldn't have kissed you. Again. I... I really need a cup of coffee." He turned away before I could see his face and ran out the door.

I stood there motionless, unsure of how to react. That was out of nowhere. Or was it? My mind started to buzz with everything it could mean. Did he have feelings for me, or was it just an accident? If he did mean to do it, would that mean something would start between us? Did I actually want something to start between us?

I had no idea, and I knew that I needed a shower and a coffee before I thought about it at all.

~

As I slipped into the shower, my hand immediately went between my legs. I needed release...

Cee wraps his hands around me, his hands gripping my sides as we kiss. He leans down, those violet eyes staying open as we make out. Suddenly, he's got a handful of shampoo, washing the tangles out of my hair...

I jerked myself out of my fantasy. After sleeping on the floor, I'd need extra time to brush all these tangles out of my hair. I sighed as I quickly washed and rinsed my hair, then hopped out. Release would have to wait until I had a little private time this evening, maybe with the vibrator again.

I stared at my face in the mirror. Even after I thought I had washed my face, eyeliner and mascara ringed my eyes and I looked like a punk rocker three days after a concert. I even had a dried drool spot left on the right side of my face. Hot stuff.

If only Cee had been in the shower with me, I thought. *He would have told me that my face was a mess. Or cleaned it up for me...*

How could Cee think I looked even remotely close to good? I attacked my hair with a brush, ignoring the protest of my scalp whenever I hit a new knot. After I was satisfied that my hair wasn't a complete mess, I headed back downstairs to see Ben sitting at the counter eating his cereal.

"Morning, honey," I said, pouring a cup of coffee. I had

never been more thankful for an automatic brewer. "You just get up?"

"Yeah," Ben answered, focusing on his cereal. I let out a slow sigh of relief. He hadn't seen me sleeping on Cee's lap. I had no idea how I would explain that away to him.

I grabbed a PowerBar and ate it greedily. My stomach was happy to have something in it. I looked at my watch – it was almost eight o'clock. I hoped Cee would be back soon. I started pacing back and forth, hoping that our falling asleep last night hadn't made him run away. I knew how much this job meant to him, and how he treated it so professionally. Plus, he meant so much to Ben. Each second that ticked by on the clock felt like hours. I kept looking out the door.

Finally, his car pulled up and he jumped out and jogged up. Even though he'd only had a few minutes to shower, he looked like he stepped out of a surfing magazine. His hair was still damp, but styled. He'd put on his signature board shorts and a tight tank top that allowed me to count his abs. I hastily looked away, not wanting to be caught staring. I had to get my mind on other things, like work, or shoes, or anything. My lower extremities were reminding me how long it had been since the last time I had sex.

"Hey, sorry I'm late, I hit every red light here," he said with a smile, running a hand through his hair. I tried my best not to make eye contact.

"Not a problem." I waved my hand dismissively, even though I knew I was going to be late to work. I had this strange idea that if I looked at him, Ben would know something was up.

I grabbed my keys and kissed Ben on the head. "I'm out of here. Bye, Ben," I said, walking quickly and avoiding Cee's gaze. I knew I was blushing, and the last thing I wanted was to discuss our kiss, or anything remotely close to it, in front of Ben. So instead, I just took off running for work.

It was the Friday from hell. I didn't know if it was the lack of sleep, or the fact that every muscle in my body ached from sleeping on a cramped couch, but I was not a happy camper. I was too old to do that. I made a mental note that I needed to add pillows to that couch. It didn't help that I was crazy busy. I was ready to yank my hair out by lunchtime. The only thing that kept me sane was remembering it was Friday, and replaying that kiss on the cheek.

He had kissed me. I had kissed him. What was going on between us?

I was having a vending machine sandwich for my late lunch when my cell started buzzing. It was Richard. I prepped myself for a fight.

"Hello?"

"Hey, Jes, I'm sorry to bother you at work. I was wondering if it would be possible to take Ben this weekend? I know it isn't my weekend, but I'd love to take him to a professional lacrosse game and spend some quality time with him."

I was shocked. He was actually being civil with me over the phone. "Um...sure, not a problem. I think Ben would love it. I'll call Cee and let him know that you'll be over to pick him up. What time are you thinking? Five?" I asked. Maybe he really was turning over a new leaf in regards to his son.

"Five works perfect." Richard hung up the phone.

I sat there for a moment, trying to think about what I should do next. Before my mind had finally decided on what to do next, I got a call on my cubicle phone.

"Hi, Jes, this is Steve. I was wondering if you had sent over the reports that I asked for last week?" Steve asked. My stomach dropped. I could feel the panic start to make my heart to beat out of my chest. I had forgotten about the report. I filed it away early last week and hadn't done it yet.

"Hi, Steve. Yes, I remember seeing it. I'll send it to you shortly. I think my email might have corrupted the file," I lied. I knew I could send it to him before too long. I would rather fib than have to deal with being reprimanded, given how awful this day has been.

"Oh, no problem. That's been happening to me, too. Just try and get it to me before end of business today. Thanks!" Steve hung up the phone.

I looked at my watch to see it was one o'clock. I opened my email and started creating the spreadsheet, thinking only of keeping my job and forgetting that I needed to call Cee about Ben.

CHAPTER 14

*F*inished. I saved it and clicked send. The clock said it was almost four o'clock. I let out a breath. That was a close one. I only had a half hour left till I got to end my day and see Ben. *Ben.* He was going with his Dad for the weekend and I had forgotten to tell Cee. I grabbed my phone, pressed my speed dial and waited for it to connect.

"Hi, Jes," Cee answered smoothly. The way he said my name sent a shiver up my spine, and I instantly thought of waking up beside him.

"Hi, Cee. I'm so sorry that I didn't tell you sooner, but Ben's dad called me. He wanted to take him for the weekend, and I said he could, so he'll be there at five." I pressed my fingers into the bridge of my nose, trying to make my brain keep everything straight. It was hard, though, remembering the quick kiss from this morning.

"Not a problem. Glad he took our advice seriously."

"Could you please help him pack a bag for the weekend?" I asked. "He has his lacrosse game tomorrow and he's going to a professional lacrosse game as well."

"Sure, not a problem. I'll help him pack now. We were just making dinner."

"Don't worry about finishing it," I said. "I can just eat take-out tonight, since it will just be me."

"Okay. Please don't pick up anything. We'll see you in a little bit." He hung up the phone. I was unsure if it was just me, but he sounded a little disappointed. I shook it off as I gathered up my stuff and headed out the door. I wanted to be able to catch Ben before he left.

As I pulled up to the house, I saw Richard's gleaming BMW. He always kept it in such pristine condition. I always used to joke that he loved that car more than me. As I looked at how beautiful he kept it and how he let our relationship fall into the mud, I knew it was true. Ben, Richard, and Cee were all standing at the door as I came up the driveway.

"Thanks for letting me go with Dad this weekend," Ben said as he beamed at me. I knew he was excited to spend time with his Dad, and I was glad that Richard had kept a promise. Maybe this was the first step to helping Ben get his father back.

"You have fun, and don't stay up too late tonight. Remember, you have a game in the morning. I'll see you there tomorrow." I bent down and kissed him. He grimaced, and I knew he thought mom kisses were "uncool."

I nodded toward Richard and watched them get into his car. It had been months since Richard took Ben for an overnight. I grinned at the thought of the sudden freedom. I could go order some sushi, which Ben hated, and watch some of my trashy TV.

Richard's car purred to life and the two of them disappeared out of the driveway. I turned toward the door and saw Cee staring at me. He rapidly looked away.

"How was your day?" Cee asked, leading the way inside and holding the door open for me.

"Not too bad, just ridiculously busy. Glad to be able to put my feet up and take it easy."

I walked through the door and was met by the most amazing aroma I had ever smelt. I set my bag down gently, inhaling deeply.

"What is that smell?" I asked, looking around. I half expected a chef to be standing in the kitchen.

"You like it? It was going to be your and Ben's dinner. I guess now it's just yours. Ben wanted to make something special for you because you've been at your job for a month." Cee motioned to the kitchen. "He recruited me to cook. He was even willing to try something new. I was surprised to hear him give up his preferred menu of chicken fingers. He came up with most of the choices, actually."

I looked at the kitchen. I saw a fresh green salad with fruits and nuts in it, and vinaigrette on the side. There was a bowl of mashed potatoes with a giant slice of butter sitting in it, scallops wrapped in bacon propped up on a plate, and something boiling in the pot. The light of the oven was also on.

Cee continued. "For dinner tonight, we made garlic mashed potatoes, a berry almond salad, and scallops wrapped in bacon. The main dish is crab with melted butter." He pulled the lid off the pot and let the steam escape.

My jaw was on the floor. I couldn't believe he had made all of this. The oven dinged, indicating something else was done cooking.

"What's in there?" I asked, wondering what other amazing thing he had created.

"Oh, I forgot about that." He opened the oven and pulled out a cookie sheet with chicken fingers on it. "While I went shopping with Ben, he said he would eat everything I made," Cee explained, placing the pan on the counter to cool. "I doubted it, though, so I made him some chicken strips so he wouldn't go hungry. I know kids and seafood – they don't mix sometimes."

I laughed. I couldn't believe Ben had been so thoughtful that he would try new foods for me. I knew how much he didn't like seafood, even though I did. It was moments like this that I knew I was doing something right.

"I'll let you go at it. You can stuff yourself silly." He pulled the two crabs out of the boiling water, them on a plate, and brought them to the table.

My kitchen table was set for a queen. There were spoons, knives and even crab breakers. I could tell Ben had tried to make the napkins fancy, like they do in restaurants, but they had turned into more of a folded ball. In the middle of the table were yellow roses in a clear vase, and candles. I laughed when I saw them. They were giant round glass ones that I kept in my bathroom, dusty from misuse, and of the more fragrant variety.

Cee followed my gaze when I giggled. "Ben said it wasn't fancy unless there are candles. These were the only ones that he could find." Cee chuckled as he brought over the crab. "I'm not sure that 'Very Vanilla' and 'Tropical Dream' really set the mood for dinner, though."

I looked, at the feast laid out before me. There was no way I could eat all this.

"Would you like to stay with me? I mean stay and have dinner with me?" I blurted out. "I know you usually have plans, but there's no way I can even attempt to eat all of this food by myself. I could try, but then you'd get a call letting you know your employer exploded." I gazed at him, trying to not look too hopeful.

He laughed and checked his phone. "Sure, let me check real quick. I'll make a call." He walked into the other room. I perked up my ears to try and hear something without being an obvious eavesdropper. For as much time as we spent together, or that he spent with my son, I really didn't know much about him.

"Hey, how are you doing? Well, I wanted to see if we were still on for dinner tonight? No? You're going to watch a movie with your friends… Yeah that's fine… You deserve a night to relax and have some… Yeah, I'll see you tomorrow night. I wouldn't miss it for the world." Cee hung up the phone and turned back to me, his footsteps alerting me to his presence. I made myself look busy by organizing the table.

"It looks like my plans were canceled as well," he said with a grin. "I can partake in the spread. Would you like some wine?"

"Sure, I have a bottle of Moscato stashed in the cupboard. We'll just have to put in some ice cubes in it."

"I already grabbed it and stuck it in the fridge," he said, looking a little sheepish. "I was searching for your spices, and it almost fell off a shelf and killed me. You really have no organization to your kitchen," Cee joked.

He strode confidently over to the fridge and grabbed the bottle and two glasses. As he opened the wine, it made that resounding "pop" sound that I loved so much. He carefully poured the clear sparkling liquid into the two glasses.

"Let us feast!" he declared in a loud voice. It made me giggle.

"Wait, we can't forget these." I got up from the table and grabbed the plate of chicken fingers still left on the counter. "These really bring class to the whole meal."

I sat them down on the already overflowing table. I started filling my plate with heaps of food, motioning for Cee to join in and do the same. He wasted no time, his plate piled high.

Everything looked so good I didn't know where to start. I wanted to eat it all.

"So, how was shopping with Ben?" I asked as I loaded up my fork for a first bite.

"It was fun, except Ben wanted to buy ten pounds of King Crab for some reason. He was under the impression that you eat that amount on a daily basis."

I snorted embarrassingly. "You know, he wasn't lying by a huge stretch. I entered into a lobster eating contest when I was younger, and yes, it weighed ten pounds with the shell on," I said with a grin. It was a little known fact that I rarely shared with people.

I watched in delight as Cee's mouth hung agape. It was nice to be on the receiving end of that gesture.

"I was in my early twenties and couldn't tell when I was full. A gift and a curse." I smiled and shoveled another heap of mashed potatoes in my mouth, basking in the buttery goodness. "Now, I want to know where you learned to cook like this."

"I've always cooked like this," he said with a shrug of his shoulders, like his skills weren't worthy of praise. "I just normally don't show off my gourmet skills because kids like macaroni and cheese, not smoked halibut."

He paused and took another bite of food. "When I was a kid, I helped out by cooking when both my parents worked late. I had to get creative with what we had in the pantry. We didn't always have the finest ingredients, but I guess I managed a good meal. They never complained." A smile flashed across his lips at the memory. "As I got older, they let me cook more fancy things when we could afford it. They even let me take some culinary classes at the community center."

"Why didn't you go into cooking?" I said in between bites of scallops. The juice dribbled down my chin. I wiped it away, reminding myself that I was eating with an adult, not my son. A handsome and charming adult. I picked up my knife and cut my next bite smaller.

"I got that lacrosse scholarship to California State University and couldn't turn it down. My family couldn't afford to send me to any other school at that time. Besides, I love lacrosse." He held up both hands, one empty and one holding his fork. "It was either move to California or stay in my little town and go nowhere."

"What did you study?" I asked, curious and excited to learn more about him. I had read all of this information on his resume before, but it was different hearing it instead of just reading it on a piece of paper.

"Business. It seemed like the most practical thing at the time."

"I didn't see a Bachelors listed on your resume?"

"Yeah, I dropped out my senior year and never finished." He cracked a crab leg, focusing intently as he did it. It made him difficult to read. Was he ashamed of not finishing? Or was it something to do with the reason why he didn't finish? I wanted to probe further but he started talking again.

"I really wasn't the college type, though. Or maybe I was, and that was the problem. Partied more than studied." He cracked another piece of crab, using more force than was really necessary. "Finally decided in my senior year that I needed to do my own thing and drop out of school."

"Oh." I didn't want to show my surprise, but I knew my face betrayed me. I never imagined Cee was anything but perfect, like he was now.

It left me with a set of questions I was too afraid to ask. What was he like during that time? It wasn't that long ago, but the way he handled himself now made it apparent it was really a lifetime ago.

I wanted to ask him why he dropped out, but before I

could, he changed the subject to talk about what happened on the reality TV episode we watched last night. I didn't want to press further and ruin the mood, so I let it slide from the conversation but not my mind.

$\mathcal{M}$y stomach felt like it would explode. I knew I couldn't fit another bite in my mouth.

"What are your plans for the rest of tonight?" Cee asked as he rinsed the dishes in the sink and put them into the dishwasher.

"Nothing really, just sit and watch the TV," I said as I put the leftovers in Tupperware.

"Not until we have dessert." He grinned.

"Dessert? What's for dessert?" Excitement filled my voice as I looked over at him, watching him rinse each dish, bending down, his ass firm and visible.

I already had my eye candy; what else did I need?

I knew I couldn't eat another bite of food, but maybe I could pack dessert away somewhere. I had such a sweet tooth.

"I made black forest brownies." A wicked gleam sparkled in Cee's eyes.

"What are those?" I was intrigued. It wasn't often that I met a dessert that I never heard of before.

"We start with a gooey brownie," he instructed as he

grabbed a pan full of brownies cooling on the counter. "Then, we then put some delectable cherry pie filling on it." He pulled out a can of filling and opened it.

He cut the brownies out and put them on two plates, then he placed a heaping spoon full of cherry pie filling.

"Then, we put on ice cream," he said, dishing out some ice cream from the freezer.

"They look delicious," I said, licking my lips. Delicious was an understatement.

"You have to taste it first before you start saying things like delicious," Cee playfully scolded me.

He grabbed the two plates, added spoons, and brought them to the table. I took a seat in front of one of the plates, watching as the ice cream melted a little bit against the warm brownie.

"Tell me what you think," Cee said. I greedily picked up the spoon and contemplated where to start first. Everything was just begging for me to eat it. The ice cream seemed to be the best place to start, so I took a bite of it.

"No, no, no!" Cee exclaimed, smiling and shaking his head. "You don't eat them like that. This is how you do it." He took his spoon and dove into his brownie concoction scooping up a mix of ice cream, cherries and brownies all in one bite. He brought it towards me slowly, keeping his other hand underneath the spoon.

I was hesitant at first, but opened up and let him put the spoon softly into my mouth. I closed my lips around it. It was delicious – the ice cream was creamy, the cherry pie filling was sweet and tart, and the brownies were moist and filled with dark chocolate bites. I let out a slight moan.

"This is delicious," I said. I looked up at Cee and his eyes seemed to darken to a stormy blue at the sound. He blinked, and his eyes returned to their normal light violet color.

"It's all about the combination. Has to be just right." He took his spoon back and took a bite out of his own piece.

I picked up my own spoon, and took some more. I was careful to eat it the way Cee had instructed, savoring each bite.

I peeked up from my plate to Cee smiling at me.

"What are you looking at?" I asked, flustered and unsure why he was staring at me.

"I've never seen someone devour dessert quite as thoroughly as you just did." He smiled, cocking his head slightly to the side. "I think you got most of it on your face."

I blushed. "I don't know what you're talking about." I hurriedly wiped my face with the back of my hand. I felt some crumbs fall off.

He chuckled, his eyes still gazing at my mouth. That wonderful darkness started to creep back into his eyes.

"You missed a spot," he said. He took his thumb and wiped the corner of my mouth. I trembled at his touch. It awakened a part of me I had forgotten existed

"There, just a little ice cream." He brought it to his mouth and sucked the melted ice cream from his thumb. I shivered.

"You aren't such a clean eater yourself," I said as I wiped his cheek to get rid of the brownie crumbs.

"At least I don't have ice cream on my nose."

"I do not!" I quickly touched my nose making sure that it was clean.

"Might want to check again." He dipped his finger into the leftover ice cream on his plate and rubbed it on my nose.

"Hey! That's not fair!" I quickly dunked my finger in the remaining cherry sauce on my plate. I went to rub it on his nose. He grabbed my wrist and stopped me.

"Hey, this is the good stuff. We can't waste it." He slowly put my finger in his mouth, and sucked gently. "Tasty." He looked at me, those eyes swirling full of so much emotion, like a storm about to hit. He had a devilish grin on his lips.

Before I knew it he, was pulling me into his arms, closing them around me, the warmth in them spreading through my body. I looked up at him, and then he dipped down, his lips capturing mine.

He stole my breath with that kiss, and I lost all sense of time and place. I tried to steady myself, but he was there, holding me. Keeping me steady, making me fall at the same time. I hadn't had this feeling in years. It left me breathless and aching for more.

He pulled back to look at me. The only traces of the light violet in his eyes were on the outer edges. I felt like I was looking into the eyes of a wild animal, ready to take its prey. I wanted to be taken.

"I've been wanting to do that since you slammed the door in my face on that first day." He smiled at the memory, waiting for my reaction. I hadn't moved yet. The smile slowly started to fade.

"Cee..." I couldn't find any words to say. I was still shaking from the kiss, still lost in a whirlwind of emotion.

His own smile faded as he seemed to finally realize what was happening, what he had gotten caught up in. "I'm so sorry. I shouldn't have done that." He shifted from confident and lustful to unsure and respectful. "You're my employer. I don't want to mess anything up with Ben."

Every muscle in his body was tense. I gently grabbed his hand, to make sure he wouldn't run away. My head was still swimming from his kiss. I opened my mouth and could only make an inaudible grunting sound. My legs felt like Jell-O, and my insides were starting to burn with desire. That kiss had awoken something in me, a hunger that I'd let starve for years. Before I had time to let my thoughts cloud things, I let my body make my decisions for me.

I stood up and grabbed his head, pulling his lips down to mine. His body was stiff at first, his brain still trying to process what I was doing. He pulled back one more time to look me in the eyes. They had finally clouded back to that dangerous stormy color I yearned for so much.

"Cee..." I begged.

Before his name had finished escaping my lips, his mouth was back on mine. I could taste the rich chocolate from the brownies in his kiss. He put his hands in my hair and pulled me in deeper. Every breath of his pushed into mine and made me crave him more. I couldn't tell if it was his heart or mine that I felt furiously pumping against my chest.

He wrapped his muscular arms around me, his hands grasping my ass. With one fluid motion, my body was lifted up and placed on the cold table. I grabbed at his blue t-shirt, pulling it over his head. He obliged, and stooped over slightly so it was easier for me to take it off. I stared greedily at his chest and traced my hands over the smooth outline of his muscles. The sight alone made me heat up like an inferno.

I threw his shirt somewhere, and started kissing his chest. His smooth skin was hard and even under my lips. The desire was building inside of me. I went to undo his shorts, wanting to get to the trophy that I had been thinking about for months and denying myself.

Reasons why we shouldn't do this started to pop in my head like weeds. Thoughts about what this might mean for the future started to pull me out of the moment. Before those ideas could take complete hold, his warm lips traced down my neck, killing any thought except for the desire to get those pants off. He pulled back, and shook his finger at me.

"No ma'am. I can't let you get naked that quickly," he chastised playfully.

I pouted my lip. "But..."

He pulled me back in, before I could get another word

out, and kissed my neck gently. The little bit of stubble on his chin tickled as he traced to the top of my blouse with his lips. He pulled off my silk blouse and threw it aside. Gently cupping my white lace bra, he traced his hand along the fabric to the back. With one hand, he unsnapped my bra easily and pulled off the straps. His pupils dilated as he took me in. A slight smile formed across his lips.

"You are just so beautiful. You're different from anyone I've ever met." He looked into my eyes and kissed me again, laying me down on the table. His tongue parted my lips slightly, and I let out a small groan as he gently bit my lower lip. He continued to kiss down my neck, finding his way to my bare nipple, and he gently sucked it.

He darted his tongue in and out. Each time felt like the first time. Just when I thought he was about to bring me to orgasm, he backed away. I whimpered as he kissed across my chest to the other nipple, lavishing it with the same attention. I grabbed his hair, entwining it between in my fingers, trying to pull him back to my lips, but he refused.

Stubborn. I always did like that, I thought. I sucked in a big breath as he kissed down my abdomen to the hem of my jeans. I felt his hands slowly unbutton my pants agonizingly slowly. His thumb rubbed up against the thin slit of my exposed thong as he unzipped my pants.

Cee grabbed the belt hooks of my pants and tugged. I was amazed at how easily they came off, and I was glad I opted for my pretty thong today instead of my normal underwear.

He continued to kiss along my hipbone on to my thin underwear. The heat of his mouth sent waves of pleasure pulsing through me. His hands ran up my thigh. As he traced his finger along my bikini line, skimming between the fabric and my skin, I let out a loud moan. All I wanted is for him to be inside of me. To feel every inch of him.

He pushed the fabric aside ran his thumb along the newly

exposed skin. My legs tightened at the touch. I wasn't used to having so much attention given to me before sex. I was used to a "wham-bam-thank-you-ma'am" scenario. To have this much attention paid to me let me discover sensations I had never felt before.

He continued the steady motion and my legs relaxed, letting him explore deeper. My back arched as my insides started to pulse with pleasure. My breaths came out short and raspy as each motion drove me higher than before. He moaned with pleasure, a feral noise erupting from him as he watched me. I was so close from falling, only Cee to hold on to me, that I grabbed on to the side of the table, gripping it until my knuckles turned white. With one final flick of his fingers, I was taken by the overwhelming sensation of pleasure.

"Glad you had a good warm up. Now to move to the next base," he said with a smile as he watched me shatter. His eyes were still that stormy color. Before I could come completely back to earth, he picked me up and threw me over his shoulder and started upstairs. His muscles were tight as he ascended but his breath was even. My thoughts raced, exploring everything that could happen with a man of such stamina.

I squealed with excitement as he threw me on the bed, my body landing with a little bounce. He turned on my night-stand light and gently climbed on top of me. His hard cock bulged through his shorts, stiff against my inner thigh as I basked in the growing warm sensation between my legs.

He kissed his way down and removed my panties. They made a soft swishing noise through the air until they kissed the ground near my bed. He lavished me with his lips as he made his way back up to my neck. Torture. It was pure torture to feel his cock throbbing against me while he trailed down my body, the want in me growing with every kiss.

I reached for his board shorts, and this time, he didn't stop me from undoing them. He continued to bite and kiss my neck as I shimmied them down. I finally saw it, the prize I'd been seeking. I wanted him even more now.

"Do you have a condom?" I asked, trying to tear my eyes away from the view.

"No, not something I thought to bring today." He backed off slightly. I could see the disappointment in his eyes. "Do you?"

"No, I haven't really needed them for a while now." I was kicking myself as I watched this fine man crawl off of me. That was the last thing in the world I wanted. "Wait!"

I jumped out of the bed and ran to my purse. Melissa was always sticking condoms in my purse, just in case I got lucky. I found one and sent her a silent thank you, so glad she had more faith in my sexual exploits than I did.

I held it up triumphantly and walked over to Cee. He snatched it from me in one smooth movement, and tore open the package. My body hummed with excitement, arousal brimming over me as he rolled it onto his large cock, pulling it all the way down. This was definitely a prize worth waiting for.

"Now, where were we? Oh, yes." He pushed me back on the bed and gently spread my legs apart with his knee, hesitating before pushing himself into me, inch by marvelous inch. The feeling of him against the walls left me frenzied, wanting more. Greedy, I grabbed his back, wanting to pull him in deeper, quicker. Ever the tease, he refused, taking his time as he filled me up with each glorious inch

Once I thought he couldn't be any deeper, he slowly pulled himself out. I let out a slight whimper, not wanting the feeling to go away. He pushed in even further with the next thrust and sped up the motion. I lift my hips to meet him, more of an instinct than a conscious decision, and relished each stroke.

Finally, he was all the way inside of me. I gripped his arms as he kept driving within me. Suddenly, he gripped my arms tightly and rolled onto his own back. I was surprised at his sudden show of strength, but he seemed to handle me with ease.

For a moment, I thought he would manage to keep inside of me, but he slipped out. I giggled, and he looked a little sheepish. "Almost," he said. He reached down and guided himself within me again. I felt him fill me again, and from this angle, he felt even bigger than he had before.

I straightened up, allowing him to see my entire body. I hadn't felt this comfortable with a man since well before my husband left me, but the way that Cee's eyes dilated again told me that he was enjoying the view. And when he sat up, burying his face in my breasts, I started to moan involuntarily.

With each push I felt myself climb higher toward climax. My thoughts, worries and fears fled with each splendid movement. I wanted more. I dug my nails into his back, signaling him that I wanted it all.

Suddenly, he threw himself back, his eyes closed. I knew the look on his face all too well, and could feel my own pleasure begin to crest.

As I fell over the edge of orgasm, I cried out. "Oh, Cee! Come for me!"

I felt him swell within me and his violet eyes opened, locking with mine. I felt myself enter oblivion as he groaned, throwing us both into pure ecstasy. I thrashed on top of him as he dug his fingers deeper into my sides.

My orgasm seemed to last an eternity, and when it was done, I collapsed on top of him. He was breathing hard and began to pet my hair immediately. Quickly, he pulled out of me and pulled his condom off.

My stomach was so full and the day had been so long that I fell asleep right on top of him, moaning softly as he stroked my hair. I didn't think he minded.

CHAPTER 16

I woke to dancing strands of light peeping in the window through my blinds, letting me know it was morning. I was no longer sleeping on top of Cee. My arms stretched out, searching for Cee, but found nothing but an empty cold spot.

He was gone. My heart fell. I knew last night was too good to be true. I turned over and pulled the pillow over my head. Maybe if I went back to sleep, I would wake up and realize this was just another dream.

I tossed around and begged for sleep to take me back to the dreams of him. It was too early in the morning to deal with this. After what seemed like forever, I sighed. There was no way I could fall asleep, so I propped the pillow behind my head. The stinging sensation of tears forming in my eyes made me sniff, futilely trying to head them off.

How could I have been so stupid?

I pulled my hair back into a tight bun and hoped that maybe the pain of pulling my hair would keep me from focusing on what just happened. I was always the fool. He just wanted to use me. Or even worse, he had realized what a huge mistake being with someone like me was. He had left me. I didn't want to cry, but even my tears betrayed me, plopping as they fell onto my bedspread.

The doorknob turned slowly and I looked up as the door opened. Cee was standing there with a tray holding two coffee cups, and a bag in the other hand. He smiled at me. I quickly tried to wipe the tears away from my face before he got too close. I didn't want him to think I was an idiot.

His smile suddenly fell as he inspected my face closer. "What's wrong?" There was nothing I could do to hide the tears still falling from my face.

"Nothing... I just thought you left." I admitted, twisting the sheets of the bed.

"Left? I could never do that. Especially after the amazing time I had with you last night." He kissed me on the cheek. "I just woke up hungry. I hoped to make us breakfast, but you didn't have any eggs or coffee. So, I went out to a bakery I know."

He handed me a cup, and took a deep sip. I had assumed the worst out of him, like I did in all men. The rich flavor and bitter notes of the drink filled me up, my spirits on the rise as I came to terms with reality. It was okay now. He was still here.

My stomach let out a loud rumble that echoed off the bedroom wall and made me blush.

"I take it you worked up an appetite too," Cee said with a smile.

He sat down in the bed next to me and pulled out a large napkin to spread on top of the black and white bedspread. He hauled all sorts of things out of the bag.

"We have a chocolate filled croissant," he said as he laid a light brown croissant on to the napkin. "Also, there's a blueberry muffin. I grabbed us some eggs, and potatoes." He placed a carton onto the napkin. "And finally some bacon. The best in town."

I took in the breakfast feast in front of me, in awe of Cee's considerate nature.

"Dig in!" he said. He handed me a fork and smiled.

I greedily grabbed the chocolate croissant and took a bite. It was buttery, flaky, and the chocolate melted in my mouth. Cee smirked as he watched me eat.

"What?" I asked, raising my eyebrows.

"You just make wearing your food so damn attractive." He leaned over and kissed the side of my mouth. "You taste sweeter than the croissant."

"Are you always such a cheese in the morning?"

"The cheesiest." He grinned and took a bite of muffin.

We polished off all of the food he brought in no time. I leaned back, feeling very satisfied. I checked the clock. It was already nine. Ben's game would be starting soon.

"Ben's game is in about two hours. I better get cleaned up." I started to get out of bed, and stretched out my legs from their folded position.

"I don't know, dirty suits you pretty well," Cee said, winking at me.

"And there's that cheese again. Might want to get some bread to put it on." I walked toward the bathroom. I looked around the floor and took note of where my thong lay on the floor. I tossed it into the laundry bin. Couldn't leave that just lying around.

"Could you walk a little slower? I'm enjoying the view." He leaned back into the bed putting his hands behind his head. It made his muscles stand out across his chest even more.

"I spend one night with you and you get like this?"

"Well, we did spend the night on the couch together. And,

I assure you, I've always been like this. I'm just good at hiding it."

"Really?" I asked, a wry smile on my face.

"Well why don't I show you?" He stood before me, towering over me as he grabbed me and lifted me up, over his shoulder. I felt weightless as he controlled me, leaving me no choice but to hang on for dear life.

Carrying me into the bathroom, Cee set me on the sink. My skin made a little slapping noise as my butt met the hard surface. I let out a little yelp at the cold tile pressed against my bare skin. A chuckle escaped his lips and he pulled me into a deep kiss.

Two could play at that game, I thought. I grabbed at his shorts and tore them off, delighted to strip off all his clothes, one piece at a time.

His kiss became much more primal, the passion of it overflowing as his teeth scraped against my lip. He possessed me with his touch, leaving me breathless. I felt his hard shaft through his boxers, the heat of it flooding me with memories from last night. My body responded to his, and I knew he would find me wet and wanting.

Cee stepped back and grabbed a condom from his pocket. He leaned over and opened the glass door to the shower. He turned on the waterfall head, the hot stream running over the black tile.

I looked at him with wide eyes. "I've never done it in the shower before," I said, a little nervous about trying sex in a new location with such a new lover. For having had a kid, I had never had a lot of adventurous sex.

"You don't know what you're missing, Jes. I want you in here. Let me show you how it's done." he said with a cocky smile. His eyes took on the dark violet of desire.

Steam billowed out of the shower as he pulled on the condom. It was like the backdrop of a sexy movie, one created in my dreams. I went to get off the counter and he stopped me. He picked me up and carried me into the shower, the door closed softly behind him. My back pressed against the cold tile, sending a tingle up my spine as his hot mouth made his way down my neck.

I eagerly accepted each kiss, and my body hummed with anticipation as the intensity of my hunger grew. His strong arms lowered me onto him, slow and steady, until he was in me and I was filled with that throbbing shaft.

I gasped out in pleasure and gripped his muscular arms. He rocked his hips back and forth, letting out a soft grunt with each push. I was overcome with sensations from my head to my toes.

I thought back to one of the first times I had fantasized about Cee in this shower. This was so much better than my deepest desires. I thought about my own fingers touching myself. As if he could read my mind, Cee's own fingers went to my clit, touching me softly.

I was so far beyond aroused that it was ridiculous. I let out a low moan, my body trembling as my orgasm washed over me. Wave after wave of pleasure rolled over me as the water continued to wash over me. I could feel my body clamp down on his rod.

Suddenly, his fingers stopped massaging my clit. I cried out as my orgasm subsided, but then I felt him swell within me. He gripped me even more tightly as he buried his face in my shoulder.

"Yes, come for me," I moaned in his ear.

He held me tightly as he pounded into me, and then he thrust deeply and stayed there. I felt him shudder as he came, and I loved every moment of it. With a final thrust, he finished. We were both breathing hard as he continued to hold me closely to his body.

Finally, he slowly set me down on the ground. I had

forgotten he had been holding me this entire time. He took the condom off and quickly tossed it out of the shower. I giggled.

"Well," I said.

"Well," he said back. "How much time do we have until Ben's game?"

I looked at my watch. "There's still another hour and a half."

He smiled and reached past me, grabbing my shampoo. "How about a hair wash?" he asked.

I could barely believe my ears. This sexy man wanted to wash my hair? How could I say no? I nodded my head. He squirted some shampoo into his hands and began to run them through my hair, sending shivers through my entire body.

I found a little piece of heaven inside that shower.

CHAPTER 17

"*D*o you want to go to the game with me?" I asked as I dried off my hair with the towel. I didn't want our time together to be over yet.

"Sure," he agreed. "Let me grab some clothes at my apartment. I'll be right back."

He tossed the towel into the hamper, leaving him standing bare assed to me. I watched as he leaned down and pulled on his shorts from last night. I stared openly, taking it all in, since I didn't know when the next time I would see him in his full glory.

I watched as he left the bedroom and listened for the door to slam. Once I was sure that he left I jumped back into the shower and shaved my legs. I always hated doing it in front of people, but knew that I was going to wear shorts today.

With my hair in a sopping wet bun, and my oversized jersey on, I went downstairs to look at the mess we made last night.

There were still dirty dishes on the table, and shirts strewn about. My cheeks reddened as I found my bra perched on top of the flowers. I hurriedly dropped the dishes into the sink and collected the clothes to toss into the hamper. The incriminating evidence of what happened last night needed to be hidden. I wanted to keep it as our little secret. As I put the chairs back, Cee knocked on the door.

"Whose car do you want to take?" I asked, as I threw my purse over my shoulder.

"Could we take mine?" Cee motioned toward the driveway with his head. "I already have it running."

"Sure." I followed behind him to a little rust bucket that looked like it had seen a few thousand miles too many.

He walked to the passenger side and opened it, allowing me to slide in. I still couldn't believe he opened doors for me. While the car wasn't much to look at, the inside of the car was pristine. It smelt like him, warm, clean and just a hint of grass. I inhaled deeply enjoying being surrounded by him.

We sat in silence for a few moments, as thoughts ran through my mind. I wanted to make sure what I was about to say came out as clearly as possible.

"Could we come up with a game plan?" I asked as Cee was turning out of the neighborhood.

"A game plan?" Cee responded, a touch of confusion in his voice. His eyes darted toward me for a moment to evaluate, but returned quickly to his task of driving.

"Yes, I mean, I don't want to send Ben mixed signals. I think it might be best if we keep what we did between us for now." The words came out in a jumble. I started to make a sound again, wanting to clarify what I just said.

He grabbed my hand and gave it a gentle squeeze. "I completely understand. Ben's emotional state is the most important priority, and too much, too quick, would just be confusing."

I squeezed his hand back, so thankful that he understood what I had said and didn't take it personally. He really did care about Ben. Knots formed in my stomach as we continued to drive. I couldn't grasp what bothered me, but I also couldn't shake the uneasy feeling growing in the pit of my belly.

We reached the field as the team was warming up, and I could see Ben, on the far side, stretching out near the goal. I hopped out of the car and walked towards Richard, who was standing on the opposite side of the field. He saw me and smiled, giving me a slight wave, seemingly transformed. A flinch of shock passed over his face in seeing Cee, but he quickly covered it up with a tight smile.

"Hi," I said pleasantly to Richard. After last night, I could conquer anything.

"Hi, I didn't realize you would be here too," Richard said, looking at Cee. He seemed still be wary of him after their last encounter.

"I wanted to see Ben's game today. He was really looking forward to using some of the skills I taught him during our practice, and he wanted to see what I thought," Cee said nonchalantly.

"How was time with Ben last night? I didn't get any texts so you must have had fun." I wanted to try and redirect the tension somewhere else.

"We did. We went and got some pizza. Then we saw that movie he wanted to see, the one about the superheroes."

"Sounds like a blast," Cee said.

We stood in awkward silence waiting for the game to start, and I debated about grabbing an iced Americano before the game, but the line was a mile long. My skin crawled with each silent second that ticked by, looking for any distraction I could find.

I decided that concentrating on my son was the only way I could ignore the awkward tension between the two men, so I took a big breath to try and focus on Ben's warmup. The men seemed to be unfazed by the quiet, staring at their shoes or at Ben, but making sure to not look at each other. Luckily, the whistle blew and we all let out a breath of relief as now we had something to focus on other than avoiding each other's eyes.

I could feel my shoulders relax, the tension dissipating as we watched the team race back and forth. Ben was on his game today. He saved eight of his ten shots on goal. We cheered with each save and I felt my voice start to go raw as I yelled with excitement. Even Richard yelled words of encouragement when Ben made a save. When the half ended, Ben ran to us.

"Hi, Mom!" Ben yelled. I wanted to bend over and give him a hug, but knew that he would hate that. I gave him a high five, instead. "Cee came too! Awesome!" He gave him a fist bump.

"You're awesome. Ben!" Richard exclaimed fist-bumping Ben as well.

Ben beamed. I could see how happy he was that his dad was there.

"Hey, Ben, let's huddle up!" the coach yelled. Ben ran back to the huddle with a grin on his face.

I touched Richard on the shoulder. "Thank you so much for coming. I haven't seen Ben this happy a long time." It was hard for me to admit how much he meant to Ben. Resentment and anger still burned in my stomach, but I would do anything for my son, even swallow my own pride.

"I never realized how much he loved this sport, and how good he is at it," Richard replied as he turned toward me. "Last night all he talked about was lacrosse. He actually managed to teach me about it. All those months that I ignored him, I missed it. I missed him growing up."

I couldn't believe this was the same man that'd been ignoring us for months. Shuffling us off when we tried to call, refusing to be a part of Ben's life. It was like he'd finally woken up, and realized what he'd almost lost.

All because of Cee.

It was a big deal for Richard to admit he was wrong. He'd still never apologized for cheating on me, but I was glad he could at least put his son in front of his pride.

Richard held out his hand to Cee. "Thank you for helping me see what I was missing."

"It's all good," Cee said. "I just didn't want you to learn about it the hard way like I did."

"Like I did…" I still knew so little about him. I would have to ask him later about that.

Cee ended the conversation by turning back toward the field to watch the game. I looked at him from the corner of my eye. He was looking across the field, not watching the players run back and forth. Every so often his eye would drift down to the ground and he seemed to be lost in thought.

The last half of the game went off without a hitch. I learned not to expect too much of the little kid games, but Ben saved shots left and right. The final whistle blew and the Bears had won again! We cheered as Ben ran over. I even jumped up and down with excitement.

"Nice game," Cee said, slapping Ben on the helmet. "You had some really fast hands."

"Awesome job," Richard agreed.

I smiled and watched Ben as the two men that mean the most to him praised him. I looked at how different those two men were from each other, and yet how much this one little boy meant to both of them.

I used to think Richard had shut down the prospect of my ever being able to trust again, let alone love anyone again. Then Cee came into my life and showed that he was someone worth trusting. Maybe he could knock down this wall that I'd built. Maybe he was the one I was waiting for.

My stomach twisted. But *maybe* wasn't good enough for me to take this risk. Maybe wouldn't guarantee that he wouldn't cheat on me, leave me, or break me into a million pieces. Maybe wouldn't guarantee that Ben would have someone in his life forever.

The struggle between my mind and heart waged on. Should I listen to my head and protect myself, or should I listen to my heart and allow someone into it? I didn't know the answer, and it made me nervous.

I walked over to the group and got between the two men to reach my son. I bent down, took off his helmet and gave him a big kiss on the cheek. This was the only man that I needed in my life. My head and my heart at least agreed on that much.

"Gross, mom!" Ben whined.

"I had to give you some mommy cooties. You looked a little low. Now you and your dad have fun tonight," I tussled his hair. "I'll let you two guys have your boy time, and I'll see you tomorrow afternoon." I stood up and gave a slight wave to Richard.

"See you on Monday," Cee said as he nodded toward Ben. We walked in silence to the car.

After seeing my son and my ex today, I felt like I had sobered up from last night's events. Last night had been amazing, but I finally realized why my stomach was in knots today.

Ben was my first priority and I couldn't let anyone hurt him or myself again. Even someone as wonderful as Cee.

I got into the car and shut the door, staring out the window. Cee slid into the driver's seat and started the car. He grabbed my hand but I was lost in thought and didn't notice his grasp.

My head whirled with thoughts of what ifs. What if Ben got attached and it didn't work out? What if I fell in love – would it work out? What if we didn't, could I handle the heartbreak?

Worries tumbled around in my head when we came to a stop in front of my house. I finally realized we had been moving this entire time.

"What's wrong, Jes? Did I do something?" Cee cocked his head to the side, giving me that confused puppy-dog look.

"No, you didn't. I'm just lost in thought." I paused, looking into his dark eyes. They were their normal violet. I could feel myself getting sucked in to them. I shook my head trying to break the spell.

"Jes..."

"I just have to keep Ben in mind. He is the one I should focus on. I don't want to endanger anything that he has with you for my pleasure." I breathed out a big sigh that was harder than I expected. I felt my heart sagging as I said the next words. "I've seen what happened to Ben when his father left. I don't want him to go through that again with his best friend."

"What are you saying, Jes?" Cee's voice was quiet.

I looked down and pulled at my hair, but was unable to find anything to fix as it was still secure in its bun. "It was a one-time thing, but I don't think it should continue any farther than that."

I could feel my brain applauding my actions, even if my heart ached and I wanted to throw up.

"Jes," Cee said gently, grabbing both my hands. They were warm and it sent a shiver up my spine. "I don't want it to be a one-time thing. You were not just a lay that I needed because I thought you were a hot single mom."

I looked at him, shocked that he thought I was hot.

"I care for you, deeply. I know I haven't really shown it, but I was trying to keep it professional for Ben's sake. I can see a future with you, and that's something that I have never looked forward to in a long time. I usually only worry about the present." He held up our entwined hands. "I want to make this work. I know we jumped a few steps last night, but I'm willing to take it slow. Nothing has to change with Ben either. I'll keep it completely separate. Let me prove it to you."

His eyes were big, and I could tell he really did want this to work. I sighed, knowing this was a dangerous path, but I had never had anyone fight this hard to get me. I sat in the car with him, letting the battle wage on inside me. He lifted my hand and gave it a kiss. He had just let my heart win the battle. My head was too clouded with his lips to focus on anything else.

"Okay, slow, no repeats of last night." As I said the words, I knew they were a lie. My body wanted a repeat of last night and this morning, as soon as possible. I felt sapped of energy after the conversation and was ready to go inside to relax.

"Would you like to come in?" I asked.

"No." He looked down at his phone. "I sadly have other plans for this evening."

I frowned. "Oh, okay." I start to get out of the car. He softly gripped my wrist and pulled me in.

"But how about breakfast tomorrow?"

I grinned. "Okay, but I get to cook. You haven't tried my French toast yet."

"Can't wait." He leaned in and I closed my eyes, expecting his mouth on mine. I felt a kiss, but it was on my cheek. I opened my eyes, shocked and a bit disappointed.

"You said you wanted to take it slow."

I shook my head, already regretting the "take it slow" statement. He seemed like the type of person who would torture me with my own words. Somehow, I was looking forward to it, though.

I watched from the window as Cee drove away. I decided to keep myself busy and cleaned the leftover dishes. I made sure all the evidence from last night was either in the washing machine or dishwasher. As the sun started to set, my stomach let out a low grumble, reminding me it was time to eat. I'd gotten so involved in cleaning I'd forgotten what time it was.

It was time to order some sushi, I thought excitedly.

As I pulled out my cell, I noticed a text. It was from Cee.

> *I know the rule is to wait to text or call a girl for at least three days, but I couldn't wait that long. Just wanted to wish you a relaxing night. I'll see you tomorrow bright and early. Remember, you don't have any coffee.*

I smiled as I read it over and over again. He was definitely trying. Now to see if he would keep it up, was the real question.

At about eleven o'clock and feeling full of sushi, I headed upstairs. I gave my face a quick wash and switched into a pair of oversized shorts and a shirt with a few holes in it. As I crawled into bed, and noticed how large it was without someone else in it, I rolled onto the side Cee had slept on. It still smelled of his cologne. I brought the sheets around my neck, and sunk into a peaceful slumber, hoping I wouldn't have to resort to dreaming about him for much longer.

CHAPTER 19

With a late start to the morning, I zoomed to the nearest supermarket, and grabbed bread, eggs, bacon and coffee. Luckily, it was early enough that the Sunday shoppers hadn't arrived yet, so no one saw me in my random, grab-anything outfit. Once back home, I only had a few minutes before Cee showed up. I started making the French toast.

I dipped the bread in egg mixture, then coated it in some Choco-crunch cereal from the cupboard before frying it on the stove. I also added a large dash of cinnamon to each piece of bread to give it that extra kick. The kitchen warmed up from the stove and I removed my sweater, so that I was just in the shirt I went to bed in.

There was a knock at the door and Cee waved at me through the glass. I gestured him in with an egg-soaked hand. He came in wearing a pair of gym shorts and a cutout tee of his old alma mater. His shirt was still in good condition and it made me realize just how young he really was. All of my college shirts were ripped to shreds years ago.

He also had stubble all across his face, which was much

redder than his hair. All I wanted to do was rub my hand over the rough hair and let it tickle my neck.

"Good morning," I said cheerily. Even though I was still unsure about this whole seeing each other prospect, it was undeniable that he always put me in a better mood when he was around.

"Good morning," he replied. His voice seemed husky with sleep.

"Sorry I'm not more dressed. I ran a bit late this morning." I blushed a little.

"No worries, my suit was out at the dry cleaners so I thought I would be a bit more casual today," he teased.

I giggled at him. "We are going to have chocolate French toast."

"Sounds delicious. I didn't realize you were such a cook." He grinned, watching as I made my way around the kitchen. "Anything I can help with?"

"If you want to start the coffee, I'd appreciate it. It's there in the grocery bag." I gestured to the table with my head and dropped another piece of bread in the batter.

"Not a problem." He grabbed the coffee and gently put his hand on my waist to scoot by. I relished his touch. The aroma of beans filled the air as he dumped the coffee grounds in the coffee maker. I heard the click of the machine and felt Cee move behind me again. He made his way to the kitchen table and sat down facing me. His eyes were following my every move.

"What are you staring at?" I asked. I felt bare under his eyes.

"I know you wanted to take things slow again, but you're giving me a bit of a peep show. And I'm thoroughly enjoying it." He pointed at my shirt. I looked down to where he pointed and turned cherry red. My holey shirt had stretched out since I washed it. The little hole near my arm had expanded to reveal the entire side of my breast. I put my arms down trying to hide the hole.

"I hope you didn't go out in that shirt."

"I did, but luckily I had a sweater on top of it." I felt the blush creep down to my fingertips as I tried to remember the past two hours, to make sure I didn't give any one else an early morning surprise.

He let out a chuckle. "I had to work hard to get a view like that, and then I find out you're giving it away for free?"

"You're enjoying this entirely too much," I huffed at him while rinsing my hands off in the sink. I went to the laundry room and grabbed an old shirt with a giant Hello Kitty on it. I groaned, knowing that it was the only clean shirt I had left, and threw it on. I tossed the holey shirt into the trash.

"Better?" I walked back in, raising up my arms and doing a spin.

"No, I enjoyed the view. It made watching you cook much more exciting." Cee pouted his lower lip out. "But I mean I do like seeing your big, giant… cat."

"Now I guess you'll have to partake in meaningful conversation."

"Ugh." He made a disgusted face. "You probably want to know about my hopes and dreams."

"I'm not getting that crazy. Let's start with something simple. Cats or dogs?" I tossed the bacon onto the skillet. It made a hissing sound as I prodded it with my fork.

"Dogs." He leaned back in his chair. "You?"

"Both. I haven't had one in years, though. Richard was allergic to animals. I've always wanted a little lab, or a mutt of some sort," I explained. "Now, your turn to ask a question."

"Favorite food?"

"Anything with bacon, or chocolate."

"I like those. It may be strange, but I love chocolate, too. I love sweets, which is a problem if I want to keep my girlish figure," Cee joked, grabbing his non-existent love handles. I rolled my eyes at him. I wished I had his young metabolism.

We bantered, questioning each other back and forth, learning all we could. I learned that he loved the beach, but didn't know or like to surf because the ocean actually scared him. It was hard for him to move so far away from his family when he started college, and he enjoyed his college days a little too much.

I told him how I met Richard just out of high school, and how sunflowers were my favorite flower. He found out about my college, and that I graduated with a degree in Accounting. I told him how I'd never really used my degree before now, because I'd gotten married and pregnant soon after.

"What made you guys separate?" Cee asked, taking a sip of his coffee.

I squirmed as I scrambled the eggs. That question always made me uncomfortable.

"He cheated on me." I focused on the eggs to try and avoid his gaze. Cee sat there silent until I continued. "He was running around with his secretary for almost a year. I guess we had hit a dry spell after Ben was born. I never realized it, but he was making sneaky texts and phone calls. Then I walked in on him."

I looked up from the pan. Cee's eyes were on me, taking in every word that I said.

"I didn't want to make a snap decision about the guy after our first meeting," Cee said. "He is a jackass, though." he said. I smiled at the comment; it was always nice to hear the same thoughts I had out loud. The eggs were ready and I put them on a plate.

"This looks delicious," Cee stated, finally breaking the silence. He looked admiringly as I added plates of French toast and bacon in front of him.

"Dig in. I want to see what you think. It's been a long time since I've made anything for someone other than Ben."

We both filled up our plates. Cee took the maple syrup and doused his French toast in it. That man really did like his sweets. He took his fork and dug in for his first bite. I watched, biting my lip in anticipation for his reaction. He closed his mouth around the bite, and suddenly let out a cough. His lips puckered as if he ate something sour. He quickly swallowed the bite and then took a big chug of coffee.

"What do you think? Did I put too much cinnamon?" I hoped that I had impressed him with my cooking skills.

"No it... it's good. Just what spices you did you put in here? It is um, a taste that is unique." He looked down at his plate and shoveled a few more bites into his mouth, swallowing them whole.

"MMMM," he groaned, convincing absolutely no one.

"Nothing crazy, just cinnamon and some sugar." I was confused I grabbed a bite of the toast and immediately spit it out. "This isn't good at all, you liar. This is awful! Why didn't you tell me? And why are you still eating it?"

I took a swig of my coffee trying to get the taste out of my mouth. It tasted burnt. Whatever spices I had used were not a great combination with milk and chocolate. There was something wrong and I needed to figure out what. I went to my cooking station to better examine it.

"I got eggs, butter, and milk," I said lifting up each item as I listed them off, "sugar, cereal, vanilla and cinnamon." Cee started to laugh, a big full laugh. I had never heard him make that sound before. His eyes started watering and he clenched his belly.

"What? What is so funny?" I became confused looking around, and tried to see what he was laughing at. He held out a finger and pointed at the bottle in my hand. He was still laughing so hard he couldn't breathe. His face turned red as he tried to catch his breath. I looked at the bottle in my hand. It wasn't cinnamon. It was identical to the shaker I kept my cinnamon in, but it was paprika marked with a "hot" label.

"What the heck? I have no idea how this got into my spice shelf. I've never used paprika before. What do you even use this for?" I opened it up and smelt it. It was warm, smoky and had a kick of spice behind it.

Cee was still laughing as he wiped tears from his eyes. "I bought it for the deviled eggs I made the other week. I know you like things spicy, so I got the hot paprika."

Wow, I felt dumb. I really hadn't been in the kitchen for a long time. I glanced at Cee, who looked like he was going to fall over due to lack of oxygen. His laughter was contagious, and I felt a chuckle escape my lips. It grew louder as I giggled at myself, at Cee, and about the fact that he wanted to impress me so he continued to eat the awful tasting French toast so I wouldn't feel bad. I grabbed at a stitch in my side that formed. I hadn't laughed this hard in years. After a few more wonderful minutes of sniggering, we both regained our composure.

I marched to the table, and grabbed all the French toast off our plates and hurled it right into the trash.

"Hey, I was going to eat that!" Cee protested.

"It looks like we'll just have eggs and bacon."

"You didn't put spices in anything else?" He looked at me, questioning as he poked his fork into his pile of eggs.

"No, it's good. I just put salt," I stated. Cee raised an eyebrow. "I know what salt looks like!" He snickered and took a bite of eggs.

"Now this is good." He grabbed a piece of bacon and scarfed it down.

"I told you I liked bacon. I know how to cook that at least."

CHAPTER 20

We sat in a comfortable silence as we polished off what was left of the breakfast. *Must've been all that laughing*, I thought. *Made us hungry.* It made me proud to know that I could satisfy him more than just in the bedroom. After a final sip of coffee, I stood up and started to pick up the dishes.

"What do you think you are doing?" Cee asked as he grabbed my waist, holding me so I couldn't move.

"Doing the dishes?" I responded, confused. I liked the way his hands felt on my hips. Like they belonged there.

"No, you're going to sit down and I'm going to do the dishes." He pressed me back into my chair and took the dishes out of my hands. "You cooked, I clean."

I sat as he worked. After he cleared the table, he dumped all of the dishes into the sink. He smiled while he turned on the water full blast. I watched as the water hit the plates and sprayed back on him. I snorted with laughter as he stood in disbelief at the rookie mistake. He was sopping wet, dripping water from his shirt down to the floor. A split second later, he recovered from the icy shock and turned off the water.

"Oh, ha ha ha." Cee grabbed the hand towel on the oven and dabbed at his chest. The only thing he accomplished was to spread the water around. His muscles stood out under the dripping shirt, showing just how ripped he was.

"Give me your shirt, I'll throw it in the dryer." I held out my hand for it.

"You just want to see me naked. I see how it is." He raised his eyebrows up and down.

"Just take it off!" I said exasperated, but grinning.

"You don't have to tell me twice." He peeled the shirt off his chest. I knew he purposely took his time, but I felt like it was Christmas morning and I was unwrapping my present.

No, I shook my head. *We're taking things slow.*

I still had this pit in my stomach every time I thought of being with him. There was so much potential for heartache, and I wasn't ready to put myself at risk again. He tossed the drenched shirt at me. Luckily, I caught it in my outstretched arms and avoided getting any of the icy water on me.

I flung the shirt in the dryer, and went back to the kitchen. I watched as he scrubbed the dishes. His chest was still wet, which exaggerated his muscles more. I stared as he flexed, his smooth arms scrubbing a particularly difficult pot. I wished I'd made more of a mess, so he would have keep working

"Instead of just standing there staring, why don't you come a little closer and supply me with some good conversation?" he asked, waking me from my daydreams.

I ambled over to the sink, keeping a steady gaze on him. I wanted to memorize his muscles by the end of this. Hopefully, then I'd be able to keep my urges contained.

"What do you want to talk about?" I asked.

"How it feels when you get all wet." He grabbed the spray nozzle and squirted water on me, soaking my shirt through until it was transparent.

"You jerk!" My mouth hung open in shock as the prickle of goose bumps popped up along my skin. He was devious with his use of the ice-cold water.

"Just thought I shouldn't be the only one shirtless. Probably should go toss that into the dryer." He winked at me. I stomped off, melodrama taking over as I made sure he heard each and every one of my steps.

Cold water streamed down my back as I took off my shirt, leaving me shivering in its wake. I freed my head and saw Cee standing in the doorway of the laundry room, eating me up with his eyes. The dark violet of desire in them overwhelmed me, but I came to my senses quick enough. I covered up my chest with my hands, but my nipples were already hard underneath them. I couldn't decide if it was due to cold, or arousal.

"Don't cover yourself up. You are beautiful." He walked closer to me. I could feel the heat radiating from his body.

I wanted that heat on my skin. He reached for my hands, his thumb grazed my nipple. I instinctively leaned forward as to get more contact. My own hunger grew and I couldn't keep it at bay much longer. Cee stepped closer, his chest millimeters away from mine as he took his strong arm and reached over my head. I took a sharp breath in, closed my eyes and waited for him to put his mouth on mine.

"Put this on." He grinned. He grabbed a shirt that was folded up on one of the shelves and handed it to me. I looked at him with shock and disappointment. I wanted him to take me right here in the laundry room. "I know you want to take things slow, and I respect that. I just had to see your beautiful body one more time."

I grudgingly put the shirt on, disappointed that he had more self-control than I did. Cee cupped my face, and angled it up to him. "I'm going to prove that I will never hurt you, even it takes every day for the rest of my days to prove it."

He leaned over and gently kissed my forehead. My whole body became Jell-O, and I just wanted to melt into his arms. His kiss made me feel safe, and made me believe that he would never hurt me. As I felt my mouth start to form the words to tell him how I feel, Cee's phone started to buzz and jarred us out of our fantasy world. He released my head and grabbed it out of his pocket.

"I'll be right back, got to take this."

He answered the phone. "Hello?" He strode out of the laundry room and on to the back porch, but he had left the door slightly ajar. I toddled after him, my legs still felt like they had no bones. He was on the deck with a smile on his face. I crept closer to the door to try to hear something.

"I had a great time last night. I hope we can do that again soon." He turned around and spotted me as I peeked through the window.

His smile fell and he retreated further into the backyard. Curiosity had gotten the best of me and I got caught. I turned away and tried to busy myself with cleaning up the floors from all the water.

"Sorry, I didn't mean to eavesdrop on you," I said as the back door opened and Cee came in. "I hope I didn't disturb you and your…"

"Nothing important, " he said in a dark tone that did not make me want to pry further. "Let me help you with the mess." He got down on the ground and wiped the water up with a paper towel. We finished in a tense silence, I was trying to figure out if Cee was mad at my actions and how to apologize correctly.

"Ben should be here soon, and I think I should go." He said breaking the tense silence. He stood up to his full height and grabbed his shirt from the dryer. "I want you to be able to spend time with Ben."

"I'll see you tomorrow." He seemed to rush out the door before I even got to have a hug goodbye.

The sudden departure left me uneasy, and warning alarms were going off in my head. I needed a distraction, and a long relaxing shower was just the thing. I spent time in front of the mirror, too, fixing my hair up, playing with it, seeing if I could make myself over into someone beautiful, put together. Was that what Cee wanted?

I ordered pizza and timed it to arrive just before Ben. The pizza was in hand when the doorbell rang a second time. I set the pizza in the kitchen and rushed to the door, excited to have Ben back with me. I threw open the door and gave Ben a huge hug the moment I saw him. My little man was back.

I looked up and saw Richard sitting in the car with a woman next to him. His secretary. My heart went cold, and I gave a curt nod. He had the audacity to bring this home-wrecker onto my property. Now I knew why he didn't come to the door. Ben turned around and gave a big wave. Richard waved back and drove off. I felt my knuckles go white and I wanted to hurl a rock at the passenger side window. With a big inhale, I looked down to Ben.

"Did you have fun?"

"Yeah!" he exclaimed. I could tell he was bursting to tell me more.

"Let's get inside. I ordered some pizza, and you can tell me all about your time with your dad," I promised.

Ben barely made it through the door before starting a stream of words.

"It was awesome, Mom. Dad took me to see the Riptide. He got me a poster and even had me get on the field and have some players sign it!"

He continued his banter as I sat down some plates and got the pizza ready only. The only break in his talking was to take a bite of the cheese pizza.

"We then went to breakfast with Dad and Ginger. They took me around the mall and let me get some action figures to add to my collection. Mom, you should have been there for the game, though. It was so intense…"

I absentmindedly listened and picked at my pizza as he described the play by play of the game. I loved to have him back, but I'd never think lacrosse was quite as interesting as he did. But I listened, nodding and trying to agree, I wanted him to think he could talk to me about anything, even if I didn't quite understand it. After we got him ready for bed, I remembered that I had that wonderful meal on Friday with Cee, thanks to Ben.

"Thank you again for having Cee make me that wonderful dinner. It was really sweet of you to think of me." I pulled the covers over him.

"You really liked it?" Ben said with a yawn.

"I loved it. The only thing that would have made it better is if you were there." I kissed him good night and clicked the light off.

I made my way to my bedroom picking up debris up as I went. Shoes here, lacrosse stick there. Ben had been home for less than an hour and he was already making a mess. I let out a sigh when I finally looked at my bed. It felt like it had grown since last time I was there. I crawled into my side of the bed and tossed and turned to find a comfortable position, until I moved to the other side of the bed. It comforted me to be there. I took a long inhale and was disappointed that the smell of Cee was starting to dissipate.

CHAPTER 21

On Monday morning, I heard the door open as I put the final touches on my hair. Ben scampered down the stairs, and I heard a thud as he jumped the last two in order to get to Cee.

Cee was here.

My heart pounded as I made my way downstairs. With each step, I realized that I didn't know how to act with Cee and Ben.

It felt like eternity, but I finally made it to the kitchen, and still had no idea how to behave. Were we going to play it cool, or pretend like nothing ever happened? Would he be expecting me to kiss him or be mad if I didn't? I looked around, but Cee was paying attention to Ben as he showed him his poster with all the signatures. I clutched my cup of coffee and breathed in the warm dark smell.

I wanted to have Cee look at me and let him know that I had this covered. I could pretend things were normal, but he just kept talking with Ben. I guessed Cee had his own thoughts of how to behave with Ben. Disappointed, I went to get my PowerBar and a soda from the fridge, and noticed a brown paper bag in there with my name on it.

"Hey, what's this?" I asked as I pulled out the bag.

"Just your lunch. I thought I would bring you something. You really should be eating better. Those PowerBars really aren't all that good for you," Cee replied nonchalantly. He barely took his eyes off of the poster.

"Thanks..." I said, a bit confused. I stuffed it into my purse and headed out the door. "See you guys later tonight."

I heard a couple of grunts from both of them in response. Cee was playing the "pretend like nothing happened" game like a pro. I could deal with that. It was a good way to act.

I got to the office and it was like every Monday morning. No one wanted to be there, and the weekend was too far away to get excited about. It wasn't until lunch that I remembered Cee packed food for me.

Inside the bag was a homemade sandwich with turkey, avocado, bean sprouts, and a thin slice of tomato. I looked at it, unsure how I felt about bean sprouts, but I gave it a bite. It was delicious, and I didn't mind the bean sprouts.

I continued to eat the sandwich as I unpacked the bag. He had included a cup of hummus, carrots and a little bag of chips. In the very bottom were five pieces of chocolate and a note. I started on the hummus and carrots as I read the note.

Dear Jes,

I know with Ben being back, it will be hard for us to talk like we want. In case I'm not able to tell you, you are beautiful. Especially the days when you're frazzled and your hair is a mess. I'll see you tonight, and know when I say goodbye it's the saddest part of my day.

-Cee

Ps: Do you like me? Please check

- *Yes – no –maybe.*

I smiled. This gesture reminded me just how young he was, yet he was being so sweet and funny. I took out my pen and put a check in the maybe box. I wasn't going to give in that easily. I tucked it into my purse; I'd hand it to him as he left for the day. I felt like a teenager again, exchanging notes in the hall so that the teacher wouldn't see.

"How was your day?" I asked Ben, setting my purse on the counter as I came home that evening.

"Great!" Ben grinned. "Cee took me to the park and we ate ice cream."

"Ice cream, huh?" I looked over at Cee. He blushed slightly and my heart sped up.

"You weren't supposed to tell her that part," Cee reminded him. "We had vegetables for lunch."

"Oh, right. We ate vegetables. Healthy stuff. Good stuff. Green stuff." Ben did his best to look honest, but only succeeded in looking more guilty.

I rolled my eyes at the two of them and laughed.

"Well, I should get going," Cee said quietly after a moment. He looked up at me and our eyes connected. Heat and desire stirred deep in the pit of my stomach. I wanted so badly to just run over and kiss him. To throw my arms around his neck and feel his body against mine.

There was only one problem. Ben was watching us.

"Thank you, Cee," I said. He smiled, soft and sweet. "Ben, will you get the plates for dinner out? I'm going to walk Cee out."

"Sure, Mom," Ben answered, not noticing that I had never done this before.

I made sure that we were out of earshot as I slipped Cee the note from lunch. "Thank you for my sandwich today. It was delicious."

"You're delicious," he said with a grin. He raised his hand, paused for a moment and then placed it on my arm. I loved the weight of his fingers against my skin and the electricity it sent flooding down my body. "I'll bring you another tomorrow."

He licked his lips as if thinking about kissing me, but then stopped and smiled. He shook his head and dropped his hand.

"Bye, Cee!" Ben called out, coming into the hallway.

I took a short breath. We had been so close to getting caught. It was a good thing Cee was paying attention.

Cee waved, walking through the summer sunshine back to his car and driving off. I held up my hand, waving as he went and wishing I could send him off with so much more.

"*Yes, No, Maybe?* What is he, in elementary school?" Melissa asked as she looked at the notes. There was one for every day this week so far, and I'd brought his notes to our weekly get together to get their input on the whole thing. Melissa was not one for romantic gestures, so I just dismissed her comments.

"I think it's kind of cute if you ask me," Cindy admitted as she thumbed through a few of them.

"He's really laying it on thick. He must really want to get you into bed," Tricia declared, playing with her martini glass.

"Well he, um..." I felt my cheeks redden and took a sip of my wine trying to avoid eye contact with them. I hoped it was dark enough in the restaurant that they wouldn't notice.

"You already had sex with him, didn't you?" Melissa nudged me in the ribs. She was always particularly nosy about this subject. "I was wondering why you had that extra bounce in your step and curl in your hair. How was it? Give me all the details."

"Well, um, I…" I was embarrassed. I hated to have all the attention on me. I also felt I would be bragging if I told them how amazing he was. My face heated up even more just remembering the way every glorious inch felt rocking inside me

"You don't have to tell us those details." Cindy shot a look at Melissa. "What I want to know is are you happy, and do you like him?"

I sat there for a moment as I muddled through my thoughts. "I'm happy. I actually enjoy waking up in the morning. Cee is great. He's wonderful with Ben and patient with me. I've never felt more adored by a man before. He may be younger than me, but he brings this indescribable energy to me that gives me life. Even after we did the, um… deed… he didn't change how he treated me. If anything, he seems more interested in pursuing me." As I said each word out loud the pit in my stomach shrank.

"Then what is stopping you from taking the next step?" Tricia probed, popping the olive of her martini into her mouth.

"I'm scared, I think? I can feel these emotions building up inside of me. I keep shutting them down," I admitted. I thought about the pebble of doubt that still scratched at me. I didn't want to get hurt again.

"Stop it! Why would you want to shut down such great feelings?" Cindy inquired.

"I just... After Richard, and how blind I was to the whole cheating thing, I don't want to get hurt again. Cee is also so young. I just can't see him wanting to be with an older woman with a kid. Or Ben. He's already had to deal with so much. What if this doesn't work out, and he loses another man that he looks up to?"

Melissa spoke up. "First off, screw the Dick, I mean Richard. He shouldn't be a factor in your thoughts anymore. He was an asshole. Just a little man with big issues. You need to live your life, the way you want and stop living in fear."

"Hear, hear!" the other two women cheered.

"Second," Melissa continued. "If he had a problem with your age and with Ben, do you think he'd be trying this hard to be with you? Yes, he may be a few years younger, but if he's making you feel happy, age is just a number. And finally, we all know the Ben reason is bullshit. Ben is a lot stronger than you give him credit for. He would want you to be happy."

I was ashamed that she had called me out, but she was right. I was using Ben as a shield. I was using all of those excuses as a defense.

"There are only three questions you have left to answer. Do you like Cee?" Melissa searched my eyes as she asked the question. I felt as though she was trying to see my soul.

"I... um..." I adverted my gaze feeling uncomfortable with all of the attention.

"It's a simple yes or no question. Do you like him?" Melissa questioned again.

"Yes, yes I do," I admitted. As I said the words, I felt them wash over me, slowly dissolving that pebble of doubt lodged in my stomach.

"Now, that was the easy question, this is the big one. Do you love him?" Melissa continued to stare at me.

I paused for a moment, but I knew the truth. "Yes, I'm falling in love with my nanny," I admitted. A smile grew over my lips. *I was in love with my nanny.* The doubt that I was holding on to had eroded away.

"Wahoo!" The girls cheered.

Melissa lifted up her hand to silence them. "Now, what are you going to do about it?"

I sat and thought. I knew exactly what I was going to do.

"Let me show you. Cover my tab, I'm going to go do something I should have done weeks ago." I grabbed my purse and sprinted to my car. I knew that if I thought about what I was going to do next for too long, I would chicken out.

My head had finally surrendered to the battle and my heart was celebrating its victory. I made it to my house and found Cee laying on the couch. My heart was pounding in my chest as I kneeled in front of him. I seized his head in my hands pulled him in for a hard kiss. His hands went to my hair pulling me in more. I melted into him. My entire body was alive with excitement, with hope. My lips were on fire, my brain was screaming for air, but I wanted to stay that way forever. I finally had to succumb to my primal instinct and release from our grasp to take in a gasp of oxygen.

"What was that for?" Cee asked. His voice was breathless, taken aback by the whole moment. His chest lifted and fell in big gasps. He needed to take a breath as much as I did.

"The answer is yes. Yes, I like you, and yes, I think I'm falling in love with you." I stopped with my mouth still forming around the word you. That was a bit more than what I wanted to say at that exact second. I wished I could take the words back.

The blood pulsated through my ears waiting for a reaction. He didn't move for what seemed like forever. My head started racing with everything that might go wrong in the next ten seconds. He sat up from his laying position on the couch, grabbed my hands and looked deep into my eyes.

Say something. Say anything, I was screaming in my mind.

He inhaled slowly. Then, he smiled. "I have wanted to hear those words since the day I met you. I have wanted to say those words to you since the day you first let me into your house. I love you," he said, grinning. Then, he surprised me by putting his hands on my face and greedily pulling my mouth onto his.

I was complete. Perfect. Happy. I knew my head was no longer was fighting my heart. My body wanted more than just a kiss on my lips. I wanted his hands on me, his mouth on me and I wanted to start now.

"Want to go upstairs?" Cee asked, as if he could read my mind.

I suddenly remembered my son. "What about Ben? I don't want to wake him up."

"He's not here. He left about ten minutes ago," he said. "Your friend Cindy called me and said her son wanted to have a sleepover with him. She said you okayed it."

Cindy, that devilish woman, had known what I planned on doing when I left the bar. She had made sure I was going to be able to have it without interruption. I'd have to thank her later.

I nodded my head, and he took my hand in his. We scampered up the stairs to the bedroom. Cee patted my butt gently with each step. I giggled and tried to outrace him to the bed, but he was hot on my heels.

When I finally threw myself down on the bed, I was

breathing heavily, but it wasn't from running up the stairs. I felt young and *ready*. Cee pulled me to the edge of the bed, and I let out a squeal as my dress rode up and exposed my thighs. I sat up and my hands went to take his shirt off. I felt his strong muscles flex as I pulled it over his head.

"Tonight, we are going to take it slow," he said. He smiled a devilish grin, his eyes were dark with desire. He rolled up my dress, exposing my thighs, and ran his hand up my legs. His calloused hands felt rough and hot.

"Smooth," he said with a smile, and started to plant kisses from my knee up.

He made it to my panties before I bucked my hips forward. I couldn't wait for his lips any longer, but he pulled away and leisurely made his way back down. He was teasing me. My dress came off over my head in one easy pull. I sat on my bed in bra and panties. Without thinking, I crossed my hands over my body.

"You are stunning." He whispered in my ear grabbed my hands and uncovered my body.

He stared at me with such reverence that I felt like a goddess. I relaxed and he moved in for a kiss on my lips. He continued down my neck to my left breast as he undid my bra. I swore each kiss lasted a lifetime, and I never wanted it to stop.

The second my breasts were free of their confines his mouth was on my nipple, sucking and providing a quick nip of the teeth. I let out a moan, enjoying the mix of soft and hard. He cupped my other breast and palmed my nipple between his thumb and forefinger. Just when I was about to explode, he stopped and continued his kisses downward.

He only stopped when he hit my panty line. He looped a finger underneath and pulled them off with a smooth motion. His lips lavished each inch of my inner thigh until his mouth was on me, on all of me. He ran his tongue over my wetness, making me grab the sheets and ball them.

I lifted my hips to get more of him, as much of him as I could. He grabbed hold of my butt with one hand and held it up so he could go deeper. He continued the back and forth movement of his tongue as he carefully slid a finger inside, stroking in an alternate pattern. I grabbed his hair, pulling him in. My body ached for him. I moaned as I felt his tongue and fingers move. I knew I was going to climax, but I wanted him first.

"Cee, please," I begged. "Please."

He seemed to know exactly what I wanted. He quickly produced a condom out of nowhere. I watched with anticipation as he slowly rolled it onto himself before positioning himself over me. I knew how aroused I was, how ready I was for him, so it didn't surprise me at all when he pressed into me without any effort at all.

"Oh my god," he said. "You're so wet."

I smiled and then moaned as he pulled my hands up over my head on the bed, pounding into me. The angle of his cock was fantastic, hitting all the right spots, and rubbing against me in a way that I knew would have me orgasm. As I felt myself get closer to orgasm, I wrapped my legs around his back. He seemed to understand what that meant, doubling his efforts.

I felt my body open to him, drawing him in deeper as my body spasmed. I now knew what the French meant when they called an orgasm "the little death," as my body surrendered to him completely. I was completely his.

And that's why, when he pulled out of me and turned me over, I didn't argue at all. For once, I wasn't self conscious about my weight. For once, I didn't care. I was completely his. And as I pushed myself up onto my hands and knees, baring myself to him, enticing him to take me again, I knew that he appreciated the way I looked.

I heard him grunt with pleasure as he took me from behind. The penetration was so deep that I almost told him to slow down, but I couldn't find the words. I just accepted it, accepted how good it all felt. I knew it felt good for him as well. With his hands on my hips, I could feel exactly how turned on he was by all of this.

When those hands began to squeeze harder, I knew he was ready. "Come for me," I moaned, just as before. He didn't seem to argue at all. He needed release, and the only thing I could think about was the rhythm of our love-making. I felt him swell within me, somehow becoming even bigger than he had been before. I heard him practically roar behind me, then heard his ragged breathing as I knew he orgasmed.

I lowered my hips to the bed, hugging my pillow and cooing softly as he finished his orgasm. He followed me down, panting as he put his full weight on top of me. His muscles felt so good on top of me. With the events of the day, I was exhausted, and I fell asleep before he even pulled out of me.

I woke up in the morning wrapped in his strong arms, relieved that it wasn't just a dream. My clock said I still had another few minutes until I had to get up and get ready for work, so I decided to make the most of it. I snuggled in closer to Cee, feeling his breath lightly tickle the back of my neck.

"Good morning, beautiful," Cee whispered.

"Good morning, yourself. I thought you were still asleep."

"Why would I want to sleep the time I have with you away? You're much better than any dream I could ever have." He gently kissed my temple, brushing my hair to the side.

I chuckled. He was such a smooth talker. He drew me in tighter and we laid there in comfortable silence with only Cee's soft breathing dictating the passing of any time. I wanted to freeze this moment forever.

BEEP BEEP BEEP

My phone alarm started to go off, pulling me out of my perfect moment.

"Ugh," I sighed. I did not want to get up and go to work. It took all my will power to roll out of bed and put my feet on the floor. I sat for a moment and tried to motivate my body to move. As the nerves started to respond to my brain's request, I felt a chin on my shoulder.

"You could always play hooky today and just hang out," Cee recommended. His voice was like a lullaby and shut off the commands my brain had worked so hard to relay to my muscles. His strong arms wrapped around me and drew me back to bed. He looked at me, his eyes big and pleading.

"I don't know... I really shouldn't do that. I've only been there for a couple of months."

"It would just be one day, you know everyone else at work has already played hooky once," he cooed. "I would definitely show my appreciation if you did it." He started to nuzzle my neck. My will power hit the road as he kissed my ear.

"Oh, fine, I'll do it, but you owe me." I rolled over and grabbed my phone.

"Thank you for calling TrueTech Accounting. This is Daniel, how can I direct your call?"

"Hi, Daniel, this is Jes. I'm not going to make it into work today. I feel a little under the weather. Can you let Steve know?"

"Sure thing. I hope you feel better."

I hung up the phone and looked at Cee.

"So how are you going to make it up to me?" I asked as I laid the phone down on the nightstand.

"Let me show you." He brought me in for a deep kiss, pulling me into him. What I got was way more than just a kiss.

"As much as I want to stay in bed with you, we have some things to do today." Cee jumped out of bed and pulled on his boxers. That was one view that I would never get sick of. I lay there, entangled in the sheets, and feeling like every muscle in my body was humming with pleasure.

"I'm going to run to my apartment, and get changed," he said. He leaned over me and gave me a warm kiss. "Let's grab Ben and have a day at the beach."

"A man with a plan. I love it." I rolled over to get out of the bed and watched as that ass left my bedroom. I hated to see him go, but I loved to watch him walk away.

After a long shower, I threw on my go-to bathing suit. It was a one piece that was black, but had a low front and a super low back. It hid all the troubled tummy spots, but I thought it made my rack look amazing. With a pair of swim shorts and a sundress thrown on top, I was ready for a day at the beach.

Ben was ready and as excited to spend the day with Cee as I was. We headed to the nearest beach with umbrellas, towels, and of course lacrosse supplies. It took us about two hours to get there by car, but I was pleasantly surprised at how easy the traffic was. The company made it even better.

I stepped out into the sun, clutching my floppy hat as a breeze went by. The sand whipped up by the breeze stuck to my ankles and I could taste the salt water in the air. It was a gorgeous day out, perfect to spend at the beach. We laid out all of our stuff on the hot white sand and Cee set down the cooler.

"I have lunch for us, too," he said. He stood up and took off his shirt, exposing his smooth muscular chest.

I followed each muscle down until I reached his swim trunks, which hung off his hips. I gave a big gulp as my face went hot. I had seen him naked multiple times, but for some reason, he always was able to make me be hot and bothered just standing there.

"What do you want to do first?" Cee asked Ben as he poured on some sunscreen.

"Can we go practice? I haven't played in a few days and I want to make sure I'm ready for the game."

They both looked at me, begging for my approval with their big puppy dog eyes.

"Go. I'm just going to be here getting some sun. But you better put some sunscreen, Ben." I kept a watchful eye on my son as he put on his sunscreen. He always forgot and would turn as red as a lobster, and then complain.

"You too, mister." I scolded Cee playfully. Watching him rub that sunscreen all over those delicious muscles was too good to pass up. He had an amazing sheen once he was done that made him look he was about to do a photo shoot for a swimming magazine. He caught me staring and winked at me, causing my cheeks to redden further from the already hot sun.

Cee got Ben's back with the lotion and I laughed when Ben tried to get Cee's. Ben had to jump up and down to reach his shoulders. I gave them both a once over and then nodded. They were good to go. The next moment, I had a bottle of sunscreen tossed at my face and I could see the backs of the two boys sprinting down the beach. I shook my head watching them as I got settled.

I opened up the bright blue beach umbrella and stuck it firmly in the sand. It only provided enough shade to cover half my blanket, but it would have to do. I tried to lay down on the warm sand, grunting as I adjusted the black swimsuit and shorts. The suit may have been my favorite, but I still hated the way the fabric rode up. When I finally felt that I had settled and looked somewhat decent on the towel, I stuck my legs out in the sun and watched the boys. Cee and Ben were throwing the ball back and forth between their sticks. My book was propped up on my chest and I started to read.

The next thing I knew, Ben's hand was on my shoulder shaking me awake.

"Is it lunch time?" I yawned. I didn't realize I was so tired, but a nap had definitely felt good. The warm sun had lulled me to sleep.

"Yup," Ben replied, as he grabbed a drink out of the cooler and guzzled it down. He spilled most of the blue liquid on his chest. I sighed. Sticky and sand. I couldn't wait to have to clean that up later.

"What's for lunch?" I looked at Cee. My stomach grumbled as if to voice its concern as well.

"Sandwiches, chips, some fruit, and drinks," he explained, pulling out each items from the cooler and laying them out on the blanket.

"Looks delicious," I said as I grabbed a sandwich. It was turkey with avocado and bean sprouts. I took a greedy bite. Bean sprouts had started to grow on me.

We sat there in silence, inhaling our food. I had worked up an appetite taking that nap and this sandwich was hitting the spot. We got through our sandwiches and the bag of chips before we finally slowed down and took a breath.

This is what heaven feels like, I thought. I have everything I could ever need: warm feet, a full belly, a happy son, and an amazing man.

I leaned back into the sand and reveled in the feeling. Ben, never one to sit still for more than ten minutes, stood up and wiped the crumbs from his chest and shorts. He burst off to the ocean and splashed around. Cee and I both stared off in Ben's direction, watching as he giggled with each wave that he was chased by.

"This was a great idea to play hooky. I haven't been to the beach in ages." I grabbed a piece of watermelon from the fruit bag and sucked on it. The juice was sweet and dripped down my chin.

"It's fantastic." Cee reached for a piece of watermelon as well. "You really make wearing food look good."

I quickly wiped my chin to get rid of the juice, but wished it were his fingers doing the work instead. Ben started to gesture to us. I couldn't hear his voice over the waves, but knew he wanted us to come play with him. The ocean could be his only friend for so long.

I finished up the sweet watermelon and tried to remove some of the sand that clung to every inch of my body. I was always a magnet for sand and I would find it for weeks later, still stuck to me. The sand burned my feet as we started to the ocean. I wanted to get to the water fast, but Cee stepped in front of me.

"You might want to take off your shorts." Cee commented.

I blushed. I had forgotten about the shorts. I hated to take the shorts off and be more naked then I already was. "No, it's fine. It's…"

"I want to see that beautiful body," he added in a husky voice, so low that I didn't worry about Ben hearing him.

With this final encouragement, I removed my shorts. I could feel my cheeks redden more, and I looked around to see if anyone was looking at me. Cee kept his eyes on me. I noticed them darken with desire as I tossed the shorts onto the towel.

"Now that is one hot momma." He picked me up and threw me over his shoulder. I squealed like a child. I forgot how strong he was and how light he made me feel. In his arms, I felt beautiful. He sprinted into the water, splashing as he waded deeper. With a flip of his arms he dunked me into the cold ocean, the frigid temperature taking my breath away.

Sputtering, I resurfaced and went looking for blood. I heard Ben howl with laughter nearby. The salt water stung my eyes as I tried to blink them clear. My vision finally cleared and I saw Cee standing in the shallows, chuckling at my distress. I splashed my way to him to seek my vengeance.

"Ben said to do it." Cee pointed to my son, trying to sound completely innocent. I turned my attentions to my son and paddled back to him, throwing water at him as I went. We splashed water at each other, laughing and giggling so loud I swear they could hear us three beaches over. I got closer to Ben and whispered a plan on how to get Cee back. Ben nodded and we put the plan into place.

He swam over to Cee and asked him to launch him into the water. Cee obliged and wadded deeper into the ocean. As Ben distracted him, I swam underneath the water and tickled Cee's legs. I knew he would freak out, because he hated that he couldn't see what was near him in the water. He yelped so loud, I heard it under the water.

When I resurfaced, I saw Ben doubled over in a fit of giggles. Apparently, Cee had just jumped out of his skin. Cee was so focused on what lurked in the ocean, he hadn't noticed that I was behind him. I waited for a moment and jumped on him so he would fall into an oncoming wave. Together we tumbled into the water. Cee sputtered out water as he resurfaced, but eventually joined in our laughter.

It was a never-ending water battle until I finally had to call it quits, when my hands were so pruney that I couldn't tell what was fingertip or knuckle. The warm sand felt good on my numb toes. All I wanted to do was fall into it and absorb all that heat, but I knew I would have to rinse out sand for the next few days if I did. I got to our beach towels and wrapped one around me. The heat of the day was so comforting that all I could do was bask in it.

The boys finally got out of the water, too. Ben's teeth

were chattering so hard he couldn't talk. I wrapped him up in a sun-warmed towel and he could only nod in appreciation.

When the sun was low on the horizon, we took one last walk along the beach. Cee and I were side by side while Ben was up ahead, searching for shells. Cee was close to me, but still being very careful not to get too close.

I accidentally bumped his hand as we walked, and it sent a tingle up my arm. I looked at him, then to Ben, and I realized that this was picture-perfect. This was what I wanted.

No, this is what I *needed.*

I grabbed Cee's hand, enveloping my smaller one in his. He looked at me with a surprised look and raised an eyebrow. I smiled and nodded, gently squeezing his hand. He gripped mine and we continued to walk along the beach.

"Mom, look at what I found!" Ben turned around and ran toward us.

Cee tried to drop his hand, wanting to keep the relationship from Ben as I had asked before. I kept a firm grasp. I wanted to take our relationship to the next level. It was the first time my head and my heart agreed. I wasn't sure how Ben would react, but I was ready to risk it.

Ben had a perplexed look on his face when he saw his mother and nanny holding hands. He looked back and forth between us for a moment, his brain trying to understand. Finally, a smile filled his face as he realized what it meant. He'd seen enough Disney movies to know where things were headed. I'd have to have a discussion with him later, but I liked that he was happy about it.

I knew he liked having Cee around as much as I did. Ben ran towards us, showing the creatures he had collected throughout the day. He didn't say a word about our hands, but he had a giant grin on his face.

As the final rays from the sun disappeared, we headed back and packed up the remaining food and stored it in the cooler. We all tried to wipe off all of the remaining sand, but I felt like I was covered from head to toe. I knew I would be finding sand in my car and clothes for the next week. It was worth it, though.

Ben was fast asleep in the back seat by the time we arrived back home. He had a busy day today, and I didn't want to wake him, so I picked him up and carried him into the house, Cee following behind me with the cooler and blankets. With a kiss goodnight, I tucked Ben in and reminded myself that he'd need to take a shower in the morning. I'd need to wash his sheets as well. I tiptoed out of the room, and shook my head at all the sand that was already tracked in. There was some serious cleaning in my future.

"That was a fun day," I said, helping Cee throw the remaining watermelon into the fridge.

"Yes it was. Come over here." He walked toward the kitchen chair and sat down. He patted his leg and I sat on his lap. He pulled me in close and started to nuzzle my neck.

"I love the smell of you," he said as he took a big breath in.

"Really?" I murmured, closing my eyes and reveling in his touch. "I smell like saltwater, sand, and sweat."

"Sounds like heaven to me."

I giggled as he continued to sniff my neck. I pushed him back and looked at him in the eyes.

"Thank you."

"For what?"

"Everything. For making Ben happier then he has been in years. For taking care of him." I swallowed trying to find the right words. "And for me. You made me trust again, and it is so hard for me to trust. I haven't felt this way about someone in a very long time."

"I owe you the same thanks. For a long time, I had this hole in my heart. I was missing something until you opened that front door." He kissed me. I could feel the emotions I had been holding back wash over me. I enjoyed this feeling of trust. He pulled back and sighed. "As much as I want to stay, I do have to go home. I sadly have plans tomorrow."

I gave him a fake pout. "Can I join?"

He gave a light chuckle, his breath tickling my hair. "No. But I'll be able to stop by."

Cee's phone went off. I tried to grab it from him. My plan was to answer it and see who was calling him this late at night. I got as far as getting the phone in my hand before he stopped me. He ripped the phone from my hands just as it stopped ringing and went to voicemail.

"Jes." Cee growled. He wasn't playing. There was no laughter in his eyes. In fact, there was a little fear. What was he afraid of? "Don't."

I slid off his lap, the burn of his admonishment ruining the nice moment we'd shared. Rubbing my wrist, I assessed him with new eyes.

Warning bells went off on my cheating alarm. I tried to ignore them, but it was too close to what had happened before.

I took a deep breath. Just because Richard had done nearly the same thing to me two years ago didn't mean that Cee was too. Still, I couldn't come up with a good reason for Cee to hide who was calling him from me.

I silently walked him to the door, feeling like I should say something. Instead, I gave him one last kiss and just closed the door behind him. I was too afraid what might happen if I pressed the issue. The small security light outside illuminated Cee in a warm yellow light as he walked to his car and started the engine.

I wondered where he went on these excursions I couldn't join in on. I wanted to believe that they were nothing, probably just running errands or checking up on a previous nanny family, but something about them gave me pause.

Why wouldn't he just tell me where he was going? Who was calling him after work? What was he keeping from me? Was there someone else?

No, I told myself. *He likes me. He wouldn't do that to me. He wouldn't do that to Ben.*

But, as I watched him drive away into the night, his cellphone up to his ear, I couldn't help but wonder who he was talking to instead of me.

CHAPTER 23

"Am I being crazy?" I asked my friends the next Thursday. "He keeps getting texts and disappears without telling me where. And, whenever he gets a phone call, he takes it in the other room." I knew if anyone would be able to help me make sense of him, it would be these girls.

"It's probably nothing," Cindy reassured me, patting me on the hand. "You two are a new couple, and it takes time to get to know one another. He'll tell you when he's ready."

"I know. It's just that ever since Richard, I can't help but see the similarities." I remembered the late night phone calls from a number I was unfamiliar with. He would always get out of bed and take the calls in the other room and then disappear for "work." He always kept his cellphone on him, and answered texts even if we were in the middle of a conversation. As I remembered all the things Richard had done while we were together, my heart started beating faster.

There were so many similarities. I was too smart to fall for this twice. I'd learned my lesson the first time. It made my heart hurt to even think about it, but I couldn't shake the feeling.

161

"You could always check his phone while he's in the shower or something. Sometimes a girl has got to snoop. You don't want to be an idiot again. Fool me once shame on you, fool me twice shame on me," Melissa interjected. She could see I was battling with my thoughts and was trying to help.

"Or you could always ASK him about it. Maybe he has a reason," Cindy offered, the voice of reason.

"As much as I hate to admit it, Melissa is right," Tricia said. "You don't want to get hurt as bad as you did last time. I mean, I love what the man has done for you. I haven't seen you this happy in a long time. But how much do you really know about him?"

The last few words Tricia said made my mouth turn dry. She was right. I knew I was falling in love with him, and all that he had shown me of himself was amazing, but I didn't really know a lot about him. He never talked about his family, or past relationships. It was really me doing most of the talking while he listened attentively. Tears started to well up in my eyes. I tried to blink them away before anyone else could notice.

"Oh honey, we didn't mean to upset you. Cee really does seem like a great guy. We're probably making something out of nothing." Tricia put a hand on my shoulder, rubbing it gently.

"No, you guys are right. How could I be so dumb? I swore off men for a reason, and then I go and jump into this. I don't know about it now. I really have to go home and figure this out." I hung my head in shame.

"Talk to Cee, let him know how you're feeling. Maybe he can calm your fears," Cindy said, trying to help.

I finished off my glass of wine and slapped my cash down to cover my part of the bill.

"I'll see you guys later. I need to go home." The girls all nodded and tried to offer me smiles as I continued to beat myself up inside. The little pit I had in my stomach had returned.

I caught a glimpse of myself in the rearview mirror as I drove home. I had put makeup on and done my hair, but I looked like a busy, single mom. I didn't deserve a hot, young man like Cee. He was all muscles and I was barely fitting into my jeans. I sighed and pushed the mirror back into position. I knew I should ask Cee, but he could just lie. He had no reason to tell me the truth about what he was up to.

I got home and found Cee and Ben on the couch. Ben was playing a video game while Cee was texting on his phone. I tried to sneak up behind him and maybe catch a glance of his phone, but he turned it off before I could get close enough.

"You're home early." Cee commented turning around on the couch.

"Yeah, not really feeling it tonight. I'm pretty tired. I think it's time to go to bed." I kept my eyes on him and held my mouth straight. I didn't want him to know what I was thinking. What if I was wrong, and screwing this great thing up because of my trust issues? That would be just like me to overreact. But, what if I was right?

"Come on, Ben, let's say goodbye to Cee and get you ready for bed." I motioned with my head for Ben to get moving.

Cee's brows furrowed at my statement, concern on his face. Usually we hung out for a bit after Ben went to sleep.

"You sure you're feeling all right?" He stood up and put his hand on my head, feeling for a temperature.

"Yes, I'm fine, just tired. I have a long day of work tomorrow, too," I lied, shaking my head away from his touch.

"Okay, well, let me know if I can do anything." Cee walked toward the door and leaned in for a kiss. I turned so he kissed my cheek.

"Just in case I'm getting a cold, don't want you to get ill," I explained when I saw the hurt look on Cee's face.

He nodded, picked up his things, and walked out to his car. I sat on the couch as Ben put away his game.

"Ben, can I ask you a question?"

"Sure." He continued to wrap up his controllers. At least he put those away on a regular basis.

"Have you ever noticed that Cee texts a lot?" I avoided looking at him. I hated to bring my son into this, but I had to know.

"Yeah." Ben shrugged.

"Does he ever say anything about it?"

"Not really." He paused for a moment and thought. "I sometimes see the name of Ann flash by on it."

Ann. My heart sunk.

"Okay. Thanks, honey. Let us get you to bed."

I tossed and turned that night, begging for sleep to take me so I would stop thinking. My mind replayed every moment that I was with Cee. I noticed that he indeed did have his cell phone at all times, and he did text often. I remembered the nights that he would disappear, or wouldn't want to stay late. The more I thought about it, the more I worked myself up.

I had to find more proof.

I'll talk to him this weekend, I decided.

Ben was going with his Dad and Cee and I had made plans to be together. That was when I would find out if I was just a worrywart, or if I really did have a problem.

On date night, after going out to a movie and eating home cooked spaghetti, I asked Cee to stay over. I wanted some time to talk to him, and was planning to do it as we went to bed.

I tried to ask him multiple times about the texting, and about the Ann woman Ben mentioned, but I couldn't do it. I had this shred of hope that I was being crazy, and if I said something, I could be proven wrong. If I didn't say anything, then I could continue to live in my fantasy world.

I laid down in bed and Cee laid beside me. He shifted himself so that my head was on his chest. I could feel the constant beat of his heart. He stroked my hair. A cold ache settled in my stomach.

"Are you still feeling sick? You were really quiet tonight," Cee commented. He tugged out a small knot in my hair with his fingers. The sensation sent chills up my spine.

"Yeah, I'm a little out of it," I replied. I had actually been watching him and his phone and making mental notes of how many times he used it.

At one point, I left my phone upstairs on purpose and tried asking to borrow his to text Ben. Instead of letting me have his, he went and walked all the way to my bedroom to grab mine. I'd opened my heart to him, and in return he didn't trust me enough with his phone. What else was he hiding?

I finally heard the soft even breaths that meant Cee had dozed off. I wasn't the only one that was tired. I'll talk to him in the morning about it, then I'll have the courage to.

I tried to fall asleep with no success, tossing and turning throughout the night. I just kept thinking that this was all a lie. That I was going to get burned again.

I had just closed my eyes when I heard Cee's phone go off. He looked over at me, but I continued to keep my eyes closed since wanted to see what he would do if he thought I was asleep.

"Hello?" He picked up the phone with a whisper and

walked into the master bathroom shutting the door slightly. I perked up my ears trying to hear his more.

"Now? Okay, I'll be there in a minute." He hung up the phone and stepped into the bedroom.

I could feel him looking at me to see if I really was asleep. I didn't move and tried to keep my breathing steady. I heard him pick up his shirt, pants and walk into the hallway. It wasn't until I heard the front door shut that the tears started to come.

He had left me to go be with someone else.

I couldn't believe I'd been so dumb. I laid there on my bed, slowly letting the tears fall. The world was spinning and everything hurt. I had let myself get carried away with the first guy who was cute and showed me some kindness. I had finally started to feel like I was back to my old self before the whole divorce.

But now, I felt just as bad, if not worse. I could only blame myself now. I started to mentally tally up my mistakes, and could feel my heartache increase with each one I remembered. Luckily, before I could finish my list sleep claimed me.

CHAPTER 24

My eyes opened to the light shining in from my bedroom window. I looked around and saw Cee fast asleep next to me. I couldn't believe he came back. Maybe I had just dreamed it. I looked around and saw that he was wearing a different outfit then before. He started to move and pulled me into his arms.

"How did you sleep last night?"

"Okay. How about you?" I kept my voice flat. I could feel the emotions rise inside of me.

"Like a baby." My body tensed.

Liar.

I scooted away from him and pretended I needed to stretch. I caught a faint smell of perfume that didn't belong to me. It burned in my nostrils.

He stood up and looked at me with a grin. He looked at me like nothing had changed. As if he hadn't just snuck out in the middle of the night to see someone else, and then come back to my bed like nothing had happened.

"I'm going to hop in the shower. You're welcome to join in a little bit if you would like." He winked.

"Okay." I heard the bathroom door close.

I couldn't believe he had lied right to my face. I looked at where he slept and saw his phone. I reached for it, hesitating slightly. I knew what I was about to do was wrong, but I didn't want to live in the dark like I did last time. Melissa's voice echoed in my head, telling me the only way I'll truly know is if I looked. I heard the shower start and grabbed it.

I clicked it on and it was locked with a pattern. I tried to picture the motions he made every time he went to his phone. I drew a 'z ' like pattern, the phone vibrated slightly at the incorrect password.

I sighed. Only two more times before it locked me out

I tried a smaller 'z'. like motion and held my breath. It gave a slight vibration in my hand, but this time it pulled me to the home screen. I went straight to the calls to see who had called him last night.

Grace. She called him multiple times a week. I quickly checked the text messages. There was me, Ben, and then an Ann in his frequent contacts. I went and clicked the Ann name and started scrolling through.

Ann: So, have you told your new GF about me?

Cee: Not yet, I'm nervous to tell her.

Ann: What, you ashamed of me LOL. Can't handle two women in your life?

Cee: No not that, just don't know what she will think. You are the most important thing to me. You know I love you right?

Ann: Oh stop being so mushy

It hurt so much to read, but I couldn't stop.

I kept reading through the messages of *I love you. Can I see you tonight?*

What is for Dinner?
Miss you.
I'm so bored.
It was so great to see you last night.
I am sorry I kept you up...

I became angrier with each text I read. I must have lost track of time reading through them, because I heard Cee clear his throat. I looked up startled, and ashamed that he caught me. It soon was replaced with my fuming anger.

"What are you doing?" he asked, his voice stern. He was still dripping in his towel.

"I could ask you the same thing. Who the hell is Ann?" I stood up showing him the phone. He blanched and his mouth opened. He tried to make a sound. I continued to stare at him, waiting for an answer.

"Who the hell is Ann or Grace?" I asked again, getting closer to him.

"No one ... just, she, I mean..." He struggled to find words. His eyes looked at mine as they tried to find something to hang on to.

"I trusted you, Cee. I opened my life up to you. Allowed you to become a part of not only mine, but Ben's world." My voice started rising. It sounded shrill and painful even to my own ears. "You talked about caring about people while you have them in your life, but clearly you don't give a shit about other people. I doubt you ever cared for me. Just thought I was a piece of ass you could have as you worked. You probably don't even really care about Ben, either."

I was reeling. I wanted to hurt him as much as he hurt me. I had touched a nerve with that last statement. His jaw clenched and his hands balled slightly. He took in a shaky breath and regained his composure. His face went blank and he had an icy glare.

"Don't you ever accuse me of not caring. I love you. I love

Ben." Cee grabbed the phone out of my hand. "I can't believe you don't trust me. Going through my phone, reading my messages. If you had any doubts you should have come to me. Should have asked me. I thought *you* cared for *me*." He pointed his finger at me.

I stared at him. How could he be mad at me? He was the one who was hiding things. I narrowed my eyes and crossed my arms in front of my chest. "You're angry at me? You sound like every other jackass who has ever gotten caught with his hand in the cookie jar!" I screamed at him.

He grabbed his gym shorts, pulled them on and snatched his shirt. The house vibrated as he stormed down the stairs. I followed him, not done with giving him a piece of my mind.

"And, I didn't trust you? I told you everything. Just to find that you are texting some floozy, and sneaking out late at night when Grace calls. How many girls do you have?"

"If you let me explain..." Cee turned around, looking at me. We were both breathing heavily, my face hot with anger, and his was blank.

"No. You've kept too many secrets from me. How do I know that you're not just going to tell another smooth lie? You know how distrustful of people I am. I can't let you manipulate me anymore. I'm done. Leave, and don't come back. I'll find someone else to take care of my son." I pointed to the door.

He tried to open his mouth a few more times, staring at me while he tried to say something. I opened the door forcefully and gestured to him to exit. He finally closed his mouth and walked out. At the bottom step, he turned around to look at me. The icy glare was gone. It had been replaced with fear. He was finally realizing what he had done.

"Jes, I'm sorry I didn't explain this sooner. It's really complicated. Ann is..."

I held up my hand.

"I don't care, I'm done with you. I thought we were open and honest, and you weren't. You manipulated me. I can't forgive that. Don't come back."

I slammed the door shut, and the window panes rattled with the force of it. He was still out there. I could feel his heartache through the door, and I thought of opening the door up and apologizing. Letting him explain. But, he had lied to me.

Hurt me. Betrayed me.

I couldn't open that door if I was going to at least keep a sliver of my pride. My body started to shake as I sobbed. I couldn't believe it had happened again. How could I be so dumb?

I sunk to the floor and wept, the racking sobs taking over until I had no more tears left inside of me. It wasn't until my stomach started to grumble that I paid attention to something in my body other than the pain my heart. I stood up checking the window to make sure Cee had gone. I secretly hoped that he was still there.

But he was gone.

CHAPTER 25

I called Melissa. I knew she was free and I needed to get a drink in me fast.

"Hello?" Melissa asked the phone groggily, I checked the clock, it was only nine a.m.

"I'm so sorry. I didn't realize it was this early. I can call back later." I could hear my voice shake, and hoped that Melissa was too tired to notice.

"What's wrong?" Melissa immediately woke up.

"I checked Cee's phone, and he's been texting a girl named Ann. He says he loves her and missed her." I could feel the tears coming again. "Not to mention some woman named Grace."

"That asshole. Give me five. I'll be right over." Before I got another word out, she hung up.

I sat down at the kitchen table and slumped forward, slowly hitting my forehead against the table. I did it again. Each time my head hit, I hoped I would jar myself into understanding how I could have been so stupid. How could I have fallen for this trick yet again?

I raised my head at a gentle tapping sound at the door.

Melissa had arrived. I turned around and gestured with my hand that it was unlocked. She came in with a gallon of orange juice, a handle of tequila, a bottle of champagne, and a small red bottle of grenadine.

"Oh, honey." She put everything down and hugged me. I knew she would come through with the drinks. Without saying a word, she poured me some tequila, orange juice and grenadine.

"Let's start out with the hard stuff, and then if you want we can switch to champagne for a classic breakfast." She handed me a drink.

"Cheers." We both downed our glasses. I could feel the alcohol as it hit my stomach. It was a strong drink, but the orange juice and grenadine masked the potency. It instantly sent a calming feeling throughout my muscles. I knew alcohol wasn't the answer, but it was at least a good start.

"Another." I pushed my drink over to Melissa and she poured me another.

"Now this one, please take it slower." She held it back until I nodded. "Last thing I want to do is make you get sick."

I only sipped at it this time, enjoying the tingling feeling it gave. I put my head back down. The cool table felt good against my hot face. Melissa sipped her drink and didn't say a word.

I heard another knock on the door and saw Tricia standing on the porch. I looked at her, confused. She held up a bag from the local bakery. I nodded and she came in.

"I hope you don't mind, but I called reinforcements," Melissa said.

Melissa stood up and hugged Tricia. I put my head back down and listened as they busied themselves in the kitchen. The smell from the bag was intoxicating, sweet and warm.

I heard a final knock and saw Cindy with a carrier full of coffee cups. I focused on the alcohol as it ran through my system. I felt better and could finally look at them all without crying.

They brought everything out on plates. The three of them sat there and smiled at me, not wanting to break the silence. I could tell they were worried that if they said anything it would send me over the edge. They had learned from my divorce how I handled heartbreak. It involved a lot of food and booze before I would talk.

My eyes went from their faces to the food. They had thought of everything. There were breakfast sandwiches, hash browns and chocolate filled croissants. I saw coffee, rum and creamer to add to my drink selection. I smiled and greedily filled up a plate.

Food was always a good answer. I felt the girls' eyes on me with each move that I made. I was thankful that they weren't bombarding me with questions, but as I took each bite I knew they were running low on patience.

I finished my sandwich and put the chocolate croissant on my plate. I finally looked up to the girls and cleared my throat.

"Thank you. I appreciate you guys waiting till I was fed."

"Oh, we all know how you function, and know we wouldn't get any answers until you ate," Cindy said.

"What happened?" Tricia asked, sipping on her coffee.

"Last night Cee left without telling me. He got a phone call and just left. He thought I was sleeping. Then, I woke up this morning and he pretended like it never happened. He even had different clothes on." I shook my head, feeling like an idiot. "I'd finally had it and I looked at his phone. I saw text messages to a girl named Ann, and the reason he left last night was he got a call from someone named Grace."

Everyone looked at me, shocked.

"What did he say?" Cindy was the first to break the silence. I took a long sip of my coffee.

"He came out of the shower and caught me looking at his phone. He got mad at me for looking at his phone – mad at me! We got into a huge fight. I asked him about Ann, and about Grace. He said it was nothing. I asked him to tell me the truth, and he couldn't come up with anything, not even a LIE!" I started to feel my face flush again as I started to get angry. "I can't believe I fell for it again."

I grabbed some of the rum and creamer and put it in my coffee. I didn't want the tears start to flow and I knew I could stop them with alcohol. There was an awkward silence that came over the room. No one knew quite what to say.

"Oh, honey, I'm sorry." Cindy was the first to break the growing silence. She reached out and grabbed my hand, squeezing it gently.

I looked at her and smiled sadly.

"I just felt so stupid. I gave up men for a good year, and then the first one I fall in love with, turns out to be just like Richard." I felt a tear trickle down my check. Tricia handed me a tissue.

"He's just a jerk. I'm sorry we pushed you on Thursday to find out." Tricia patted me on the shoulder.

"No, I needed to do it," I sniffled, wiping at my nose. "There was something that I felt he was keeping from me since the beginning. My head was telling me no, but my heart and body were telling me yes. I should have listened to my brain."

We sat in silence for another few minutes, only to be broken by my phone vibrating. I looked at it. It was Cee. I picked it up and held it in my hand, unsure of what I wanted. I wanted to throw it across my kitchen, but that would break it. And I hated the thought of having to buy a new one. Melissa grabbed it from me and answered it.

"Leave her alone. She doesn't need you and your shit right

now," she announced, hung up the phone, and handed it back to me.

I was glad she had done that. Maybe he would get the picture that I didn't want to talk to him again. I hit the silence button and put it back down on the table. The girls looked at me, watching to see my reaction. I took a big breath in. All I wanted to do was crawl under a rock and sleep.

"I really appreciate you here, but all I want to do is fall asleep. If you guys don't mind showing yourself out, I'm gonna lay down." They all smiled and nodded in understanding.

I walked over to my couch and put my head on the arm. Melissa draped a blanket across my shoulders as I closed my eyes, and listened to the girls leave.

CHAPTER 26

I had a fitful sleep, tossing and turning with nightmares. I woke up to the sun setting. My phone lit up as another text message came in. I had five missed calls and seven text messages, all from Cee. I couldn't listen to the voicemails that he left. The thought of having to hear his voice made me sick. I clicked through the texts.

I'm sorry

I can explain

I love you

I never meant to hurt you.

I couldn't look at them anymore, and deleted the rest of them before I opened them up. My stomach let out a low grumble. It had been a long time since breakfast. I got up and stretched my stiff legs as I made my way to the fridge.

Inside was a box from my favorite Chinese restaurant and a bottle of plum wine. Someone sneaked in while I was asleep to drop off this food for me. They even included some chocolate chip cookie dough ice-cream in the freezer. I smiled, thankful for my friends and that I didn't have to figure out dinner on my own.

I tossed the food in the microwave and popped open the bottle of wine. I left the lights off in the kitchen glad to have it gloomy like my mood. The aroma of the Pad Thai filled the kitchen and I couldn't wait any longer.

I stopped the microwave, unable to wait the remaining ten seconds. My glass was filled to the max with plum wine and I carefully carried it and my hot plate over to the couch. I sipped my drink and ate my food. The Pad Thai was perfect and spicy, just the way I wanted it. For a few moments, I concentrated on nothing but the food and drink.

I didn't think about calories, or fat content, or anything but the spicy goodness filling the gaping hole in my life. One of them at least.

I patted my full belly and looked at the damage. An order of Pad Thai normally lasted me for two dinners, but tonight I wanted to drown my feelings in noodles. I had eaten the whole container.

As I flipped through some television stations, I heard a car pull up. I sneaked over to the window and peered out. It was Cee's car. I crouched low to the floor and was glad that I had left all the lights off. My insides were screaming to move and open up that door as he knocked, but I had listened to my heart before, and look where it got me. He knocked a little harder. Why couldn't he just let me be? Tears started to stream down my face.

Finally, after a few more agonizing moments he walked away and drove off. I stood up and peered through the window by the door, watching the red of his taillights disappear into the darkness.

Left on the front porch was a bouquet of sunflowers in a vase and a letter. I opened the door and put the flowers on the table. I tore open the letter.

Dear Jes,

I don't know what else to do. I didn't mean to hurt you by keeping my secrets. I need to see you in person and explain this to you. Then it will make sense. Please give me a call when you are ready to talk.

I love you,
   Cee.

I crumpled up the letter. He had hurt me too much. Betrayed me. I couldn't let him back in. The only thing I wanted to feel was the ice cream in my stomach.

I didn't even bother with a bowl and just took the whole pint and a spoon to the couch. I dug into the sugary goodness, determined to eat myself into a diabetic coma. At least then my heart wouldn't hurt so much. My eyes were heavy, but I was determined.

The TV let out a huge blast of sound and I woke up to some sort of horrid commercial about how to work my buns off. I didn't know how long I had slept. The pint sat half eaten on the table, most of it melted now. I got myself up and put it in the freezer, hopefully saving some of it for tomorrow.

It was tempting to stay on the couch, but my neck already had a kink in it. I dragged myself up the stairs and into the bed. My sleep was plagued with nightmares of Cee being with another woman and discussing about how stupid I was. I tried to yell at him, to tell him he was wrong but no sound came out. I was forced to stand in silence as he started to kiss her.

I woke up with a start. Cindy was sitting on my bed holding my hand.

"Are you okay? You were having a nightmare," she said softly.

"Yeah, it was just a bad dream." I sat up in my bed, a little taken aback that she was able to get into my room without me waking up.

"We thought you would have another rough day today. We came by because we knew without us you would continue to be a bum." She gestured at my hair, which looked like a rat had made a nest, and the stained sweats I was in. "Found you in here, but you were thrashing so hard I couldn't help but stay until you woke."

I nodded and tried to start de-tangle my hair with my fingers.

"We?" I asked. I was both grateful and pissed. I had thoroughly planned on being a miserable wretch today.

"Everyone else is downstairs getting breakfast ready. I came up when I heard you yell." She smiled gently at me, and stood up from the bed. "We'll have breakfast ready for you in about twenty minutes. Please go take a shower. You're starting to smell."

She plugged up her nose with her hand and walked away.

With a groan, I got out of bed and stepped into the bathroom, turning on the shower. The warm water felt good. It felt like it was washing away all of my pain and I never wanted to get out. Finally, the water turned cold and I decided I should get out before I turned blue.

It felt good to be clean, and I pulled on a pair of comfy sweats. I headed downstairs to kitchen where I found my friends. They were like a well-oiled machine. Tricia cooked breakfast, Melissa made the mimosas, and Cindy set the table. Another bouquet of flowers with a letter decorated the table.

"What's this?" I gestured.

"I don't know. We found it on the doorstep." Melissa topped off her mimosa with some more Champagne and shrugged.

I looked at the flowers. It was a dozen roses, in yellow.

Dear Jes,

I'm sorry. I didn't mean to hurt you. Please let me explain.

I love you,
  Cee

I crumpled up the note again and threw it in the trash. He couldn't win me over with flowers and cheesy notes.

"What did it say?" Cindy asked looking at the trash.

"Blah blah blah, he's sorry, please let me explain, blah blah." I grabbed a mimosa and took a large sip.

"Oh, honey, he really looks like he is sorry. I kind of feel bad for the guy. I mean just look at your phone!" Tricia handed it to me "You left it on the coffee table last night, and it kept going off. He called you ten times. He's desperate."

I shook my head. "We are not dealing with this right now." I looked at Tricia. "Whose side are you on anyway?"

"Yours, of course. Just maybe he has some reason that he keeps wanting to reach out to you." Tricia shrugged off my icy gaze and took a sip of mimosa. "Don't remember when Richard was caught by you? He didn't care, he was glad it was over. He didn't fight for you. Cee's fighting."

"Fighting? Maybe he should have been more truthful with me from the beginning." The urge to start a brawl myself was filling me. I was going to need to hit something soon, or I was going to say something I would regret.

"Anyway," Cindy cut in, trying to direct the tension somewhere else. "Breakfast is ready. Let's dig in."

We all sat at the kitchen table and ate in silence, since no one wanted to set me off again. Cindy cleared her throat and asked, "What is your plan? What are you going to tell Ben?"

"Oh no. Ben." I put my head in my hands. "I don't even know what do about that."

"Tell him the truth. He'll understand," Cindy suggested. "What time is he coming back from his dad's?"

"In about two hours." I checked the clock on the microwave. It wasn't much time.

"We're here if you need anything. We'll clean up and head out so that you can come up with a plan."

They all stood up from the table and started to clear the dishes. A wave of gratitude flowed over me. I had the best friends. I never would have survived Richard's betrayal, and now Cee's, without them.

"I'll do the dishes, just put everything in the sink," I said, picking up my own plate. "I can't thank you girls enough for taking care of me."

"You'd do the same for us," Cindy replied. After all the dishes were off the table, I walked to the door and I gave them all hugs. I was truly thankful for their help.

I filled up the sink with soap and water, wondering what I would tell Ben about Cee. Ben was going to be crushed to lose Cee. This was exactly the scenario I had wanted to avoid. By lying to me, Cee had not only broken my heart, but Ben's too.

Lost in thought, I was jarred back to reality by the water spilling over the sink.

I sighed. Just another mess I made.

I cleaned up everything, and ran different scenarios in my mind, but nothing felt right. When Ben came to the door, I still had no idea what to tell him. He gave me a big hug.

"Mom! You wont believe what we did this weekend. Dad bought me a bunch of new lacrosse stuff. And we got to hang out with Matt today. You remember him from my class? He wants to join the Bears team too. "

In the back of my mind, I kept praying that he wouldn't ask about Cee and my weekend. Luckily, he didn't. At least not until bedtime.

"When is Cee coming over tomorrow? I want to show him the new helmet dad got me." He grinned excitedly as I pulled the sheets over his arms, and looked into his eyes. They stared at me, waiting for an answer.

"He isn't going to come over tomorrow. Cindy said she wanted to watch you so that Jake could hang out with you. Cee has some other things to do as well." I watched his face fall as the lie left my mouth. I hated lying to my son, but I didn't know how to answer the questions that would come if I didn't.

"Oh, okay. Well, I'll just see him on Tuesday," he said with a yawn and rolled onto his side. Maybe by tomorrow I would have the courage to break my son's heart. I kissed him softly and left him to drift off to sleep.

I crawled into my bed and waited for sleep to take me. I hoped that tomorrow would be busy so I wouldn't have to think about what happened this weekend.

CHAPTER 27

 hit the alarm in the morning, wishing that I could sleep through the day. I dragged myself into the shower and got ready for the day anyway. I half-expected Cee to walk through the door and hear Ben scamper down the stairs to meet him.

I frowned in the mirror, remembering that I was the one who pushed him away. As I lugged my feet downstairs, I saw Ben sitting at the table slowly eating his cereal. He didn't have his normal excitement that he did in the mornings Cee was here. I grabbed a cup of coffee and PowerBar, trying to come up with a way to tell Ben about Cee no longer being his nanny. I started opening my mouth but the words wouldn't come out.

"Come on Ben, let's drop you off at Cindy's," was all I could muster to tell him. He got up from his table and grabbed his bike as we walked out the door. I walked him over to her house since she was only three doors down.

"Hi Cindy, thank you so much for looking after Ben today. I really appreciate it. I owe you."

"Not a problem, honey. Jake was looking forward to having some time with Ben," she greeted us.

I pat Ben on the head as he walked inside her home, placing his bike by the door. "I'll be back as soon as I'm done with work."

Ben shrugged and hurried off to play with Jake. I waved to Cindy and went to work.

I barely got anything done the entire day. I tried to write up a summary of the spreadsheets I was working on, but I had only completed a single paragraph when the clock hit 4:30. I was glad this wasn't due until next week.

I had finally come up with a game plan to tell Ben about Cee. I went to Cindy's house and knocked on the door. Cindy answered. She bit her lip and her eyebrows knit together as soon as she saw me.

"You okay?" I walked in the door. Her house was cool and welcoming compared to the summer heat outside.

"Yeah, I just, accidentally said something to Ben about Cee." She looked at the floor as she said it. Her shoulders fell. "I was talking to Ray when he came by for lunch. He asked why Ben was over, and I told him it was because you and Cee got into a fight. Cee wasn't going to be Ben's nanny anymore, so he would be here for a few more days until you get another babysitter." She paused looking up at me.

"Oh no," I whispered, closing my eyes.

"I didn't realize Ben was in the other room and heard everything. The next thing I heard was him running up the stairs and slamming Jake's bedroom door. He hasn't come out since. I was able to get Jake in there to try and talk to him, but I let him be for most of the afternoon. I thought it would be best until you came home and talked to him. I'm so sorry. I didn't mean to." I could see the pain in her eyes as she admitted everything.

"It's okay. It's not quite how I was hoping to tell him, but at least he knows." I gave her a hug, trying to comfort her. "I really appreciate that you watched over him."

"I'm so sorry, Jes," Cindy apologized again. "I feel awful."

"It solves my problem of how to tell him." I shrugged and looked over at the stairs. "I guess I better try to get him out of Jake's room and back home."

I climbed up the stairs. Cindy's house was a lot like mine, yet decorated so differently that if felt entirely like a different place. She enjoyed a bit more of the family feel of a house with pictures hung everywhere of the kids and plaques with motivational sayings on them. Her house was also a bit bigger with an extra bedroom addition on the second floor. I walked to Jake's door where a "No Girls Allowed" sign was hung. I knocked on the door.

"Hey, Ben, it's your mom. Will you come out and talk to me?" I yelled through the door. The door opened a crack and Jake stuck his head through the door. His auburn hair fell in his eyes as he looked up at me.

"Hi, Ms. Jes. Ben doesn't want to come to the door right now, so can I take a message?" Jake asked. He bit his lip, chewing on it anxiously.

"Can you please let me in? I really want to see Ben."

"Um… no, you can't come in." He shook his head, looking hesitant.

"Jake, open that door for her," Cindy threatened, coming up behind me. "If you don't, I'm going to take away all your toys for a month."

"I can't, Mom. I promised I wouldn't," Jake whined.

"Jake!" Cindy got in front of me, "I'm going to count to three. One, two…" her voice was getting serious. Jake opened up the door hurriedly, and I walked in.

"Where's Ben?" I asked looking around the room.

"Not here."

"What do you mean, *'not here'*? Where is he?" I looked at Jake. Panic was starting to bubble up in my stomach.

"He made me promise not to tell." He looked down at the ground and dug his toe into the carpet.

"Please Jake, I really need to talk with him. I know he's mad at me." I tried to keep my voice calm. If I stayed calm, then so would everyone else. This would be fine.

"He went to go find Cee himself. He took his bike and rode off a little bit ago." Jake kicked the toys in front of him with his foot. My mouth dropped.

"What?" I gasped. Cindy looked just as surprised as I did.

"I had no idea. I was here the whole day. The only time I wasn't inside was when I…" Cindy paled visibly. "I was in the back hanging up the laundry. He must have snuck out then."

"Cindy, we need to go find him. Can you help me? I'm going to call him and see if he'll pick up." I dialed Ben's cell. It rang and rang, and then nothing. I ran downstairs, Cindy hot on my heels.

"I'm going to start looking for him. I'll pull up his location with my tracker." I was glad I had installed that app on his phone. It had felt a little big brother-ish at the time, but after the last time he ran away, it was worth it.

I pulled it up and saw that it wasn't moving – it was close by! I ran out of the house and followed the signal. About a block up, I found the phone. It was resting on the sidewalk, just shy of the grass. It must have fallen out of his pocket. I was in a total panic now. Not only was he missing, he didn't have his phone on him. I ran back to Cindy's, screaming that Ben had lost his phone.

"I'll drive south, and you drive north. I'll let you know if I find him and vice versa," I instructed as I got in my car. She nodded and started up her own, pushing a scared looking Jake into the backseat of her minivan.

Stay calm, stay calm, I chanted. *He's fine, he's fine…*

I started scouring the streets, not knowing where he would have gone. I had no idea if he knew where Cee's apartment was. The fact that he was on his bike made things more difficult. It was starting to get dark. and to get to Cee's apartment he had to cross a lot of busy streets.

I banged my hands down on the steering wheel, knowing exactly what I had to do. I didn't have a choice. I picked up my phone and dialed Cee.

CHAPTER 28

"Hello?" Cee answered. I felt myself relax just at the sound of his voice, and hated that he had that effect on me.

"Hi, Cee, its Jes. Now, before you say anything, I'm still mad at you, and I don't want to talk to you." I was harsh, making sure that he knew I meant business. "But, I need your help. Ben ran away. I think to find you. Have you heard anything from him?" I was out of breath by the time everything was said, trying to not let Cee interrupt me.

"No, I haven't heard or seen from him today." His tone was cool, but tinged with worry. I could tell he was still angry and had not let the hurtful things I said go, but at least he cared enough about Ben to let it slide. "Come by and pick me up, we can look together. I think I know of some places where he might be."

"Okay, I'll be there in five." I hung up, trying to be as curt as possible. It only took me a moment to drive to Cee's house, where I found him already on the sidewalk waiting for me. He slid effortlessly into the passenger seat. He was wearing a tight black shirt and a pair of his classic board shorts. I looked away quickly, feeling those familiar urges start to take over.

"Jes, I'm so sorry. I'vee been wanting to talk to you and explain..." Cee started. I held up my hand to stop him.

"I'm not here to talk to you, I'm here to find my son, and do not want to talk about anything else until we've found him." I turned back to the steering wheel to show that the conversation was done. Cee closed his mouth and we sat in silence. "Now where do you think Ben is?"

"He might be up at the park a mile away. We used to go there to play lacrosse sometimes." Cee pointed up the street. "If he was coming to find me, he would go there first. We went there a lot."

"Okay." The silence between us was deafening, only to be broken with Cee telling directions on which street to turn on. We pulled into the park's parking lot and got out. It was a little park with a few benches and a playground. It had a wide-open field of grass and a swing set nearby. It was perfect for lacrosse and I could see why Ben liked it here.

"Ben, Ben are you here?" I shouted, trying to hold the fear back in my voice. It was dark now, and there weren't many lights to help me look around. I strained my eyes to try and see a shadow or a shape that might be him.

"Ben, Ben!" Cee joined in the yelling, his deeper voice carrying across the field.

"Mom!" I heard Ben's cry. Relief, pure and heavy hit my heart. I started running around following the voice with Cee right on my heels.

"I'm coming, Ben!" I yelled, following his voice through the dark. I finally found him in the playground. His bike was laying on its side and he was sitting hunched on a bench. I ran to him and hugged him.

"Mommy..." Ben whimpered as I pulled him into me. "It

hurts…"I stepped back to take a better look at him. He had worn his helmet, thank God, but he was cradling his wrist.

"What happened?" I let go instantly, looking to see what was wrong.

"I fell off my bike when I got here and landed on my wrist." He clutched the arm closer to him. His little voice was rough from crying, though I knew he was doing his best to be brave. "I tried to get back on, but it got dark and it hurts a lot."

I squinted at it, trying to see it in the dark, but I had no idea what to even look for.

"Let me see," Cee said gently. I had forgotten he was even there. He crouched next to Ben and gently lifted his wrist. "Does this hurt?" He pressed on it and Ben gave out a yelp. I cringed, wanting to pull Cee away from my son. "Try moving it like this."

"It hurts to do that," Ben whimpered.

"It looks like you broke your wrist, Ben," Cee explained. "Luckily, it didn't break the skin." He stood up and looked at me.

"What do we do?" Tears streamed down my face. My son was hurt. He ran away because of me, and now he was hurt. It was entirely my fault. Everything was all my fault. Cee looked at me and took a step toward, wanting to comfort me. I shied away and I could see his body tense up. He abruptly turned around and grabbed Ben's bike.

"We need to get him to the hospital to get it set. He'll feel a lot better once the doctor fixes it and gives him some pain meds." He turned to Ben. "Okay, Ben, do you think you can walk?"

Ben nodded slowly. "I think so."

"Good. I need you to walk to the car with your mom. Be careful not to move your wrist, and let her open your door and buckle you in." Cee smiled at Ben, and motioned him forward. "I'll be right behind you, and I'll stick the bike in the trunk."

We walked slowly over to the car. Ben had a slight limp and it wasn't until we hit the streetlight that I saw he had skinned up his knees as well. They were crusted in blood, and he was covered in grime. It made my stomach tie up in knots. I was a terrible mother.

I opened the door and helped Ben in to his seat, his face grimacing every so often with pain as we got him settled. Cee closed the trunk and walked beside me. I was shaking so hard I couldn't even get his buckle latched.

"Here, let me get it." He took my hands and moved them aside. He buckled the belt and looked at Ben. "You all right?"

"I think so." Ben looked sheepishly at him.

"Okay, you are being very brave right now. We'll go to the hospital, they'll put on a cast, and it will feel better from there." He closed the door softly and looked at me.

"I'll drive. Grace Hospital is better for kids, and it isn't too far away."

CHAPTER 29

"We're here," Cee stated as he pulled up to the ER. "Hop out and get him set up. I'll go park the car."

I got out of the car and followed his instructions, moving mechanically. I got Ben out and shut the door. My hands were shaking so bad, I had to do it twice to make sure it actually closed. Cee tried to give me a comforting smile, but I looked past him, just focusing on the next step of the process. I was still too worried about Ben, and too mad at Cee to be anywhere close to forgiving him.

"Hi, what seems to be wrong today?" the receptionist asked as I rushed Ben inside. He smiled at me, moving paperwork around, but looking friendly and competent.

"My son, he… I mean…" I took a big breath in, feeling the tears well up as I said it. "He broke his wrist when he fell off his bike."

The man stood up and peered over the counter to look at Ben. "Oh no, it looks like he took quite the nasty fall. Good thing you were wearing your helmet."

I looked at Ben and realized he was still wearing his dark

blue helmet. We forgot to take it off in the rush. I could feel a maniacal giggling bubbling up in my chest, but I pushed it down. It wasn't that funny and it certainly wasn't the time for me to break down yet.

"Alright, let's get you in the system. Luckily, it's been a pretty quiet day." He handed me a clipboard with paperwork. "Go fill this out, and we'll get you in to see the doctor in just a minute."

I had Ben go sit down in the chairs as I filled out his information. I had just finished filling out the insurance information when the receptionist gestured us into the hallway of the ER.

There was a nurse waiting for us in blue scrubs to take us to a room. We followedher, but I paid more attention to Ben than where we were going. In a brightly lit exam room, we got him set up on the examination table.

It wasn't long before the nurse walked in with her laptop. She was wearing dark blue scrubs and had her blond hair pulled up into a bun.

"Hi Ben, my name is Rachel." She smiled warmly and looked over at me. "You must be his mom, Jes. It looks like we took quite a spill. How are you feeling?"

"Okay," Ben responded, looking at me. His eyes were as big as saucers and his face pale with shock.

"Do you remember what happened?" She asked, filling out his chart. In between her questions, she moved around us, taking his temperature, his heart rate and all the other vital signs, and recording the results.

"I was bike riding, and I hit a bump." He swallowed hard, his eyes big as he explained his injury. "I fell off my bike and hit my wrist. I couldn't do anything with it, or move my bike."

"Okay," she replied, marking something in the computer. "Do you feel nauseous, or sick to your stomach?"

"No, it just hurts." Ben looked at me. "Where's Cee?"

"Right here," Cee announced, walking in through the curtains and standing next to Ben. Ben's face instantly lightened. The doctor looked at Cee.

"Who are you?" Rachel inquired.

"He is, or was, our nanny" I responded. My voice sounded flat.

"Is it okay that he's back here?" Rachel's fingers hovered over a phone resting by the computer, ready to call security if I needed her to.

"Yes, it's fine," I said, not wanting to upset Ben. Rachel's hand dropped away from the phone.

"Okay then." She turned from the computer and looked at us. "We need to take an x-ray first. Who would like to come with him?"

"Can Cee come with me?" Ben asked. I was taken aback and a little hurt by the request, but nodded.

I wanted to let him have whatever he wanted, just as long as it took his mind off the pain. Rachel helped us get Ben out of his shorts and shirt, put him into his medical gown, and then transferred him neatly into a wheelchair.

"I'll stay here, fill out this paperwork and let your dad know what happened. I should text Cindy, too," I told Ben as Rachel rolled Ben out. Cee walked beside him, cracking jokes about hospital gowns and butts to make Ben smile. I shook my head picked up my phone. I sent a quick text to Cindy letting her know that we found Ben, and then called Richard.

"Hello?" He sounded sleepy. I wondered if I had woken him up. It wasn't that late yet.

"Hi, Richard." I took a breath. Better to get this part over with. "Ben had an accident."

"What!" It sounded like he nearly dropped the phone.

"He fell off his bike and broke his wrist," I quickly

explained. "He's okay, though. They're taking an x-ray right now."

"Where are you guys? I'll be right there."

"At Grace Hospital." I was proud my voice didn't shake.

"Okay, I know where that is. I'll call once I'm there." He paused. "I'm glad he's okay."

"Me too." I hung up the phone and let out a sigh of relief. I wasn't terribly excited about having my ex-husband, my ex-boyfriend/nanny/whatever he was, and my son all in one hospital, but I could deal with that. Ben was okay.

$\mathcal{I}$ was putting the final signature on the paperwork when the nurse brought the two men I cared most about back into the room.

"Everything go okay?" I asked, setting down the pen.

"Yeah, it was awesome!" Ben grinned. I shook my head at him. I could tell he was enjoying this. He would have some great stories for the kids when he went back to school in a few weeks.

"The doctor will be here in a few minutes. He just has to look over the x-ray," Rachel said, poking her head through the curtain.

We sat in awkward silence, not knowing what to say while we waited for the doctor to arrive. I busied myself with straightening up the papers on the clipboard and re-reading my answers. Ben was having fun clicking through the TV stations. Cee turned toward me.

"I think I'm going to get a soda. Do you want anything?" He asked. I shook my head and looked back down to the clipboard. Cee nodded and left quietly. I lifted my head up when I heard the curtain pulled back, the doctor stood there smiling with the x-rays in hand.

"Hi, I'm Dr. Carl." He held out his hand and shook my hand. "I assume you're Ben's mother?"

"Yes, please call me Jes." I shook his hand firmly. At least I wasn't shaking anymore. "How are you doing, Ben?" Dr. Richmond asked, turning his attention to Ben.

"Alright." Ben shrugged. "It still hurts."

"The medicine should kick in pretty soon," the doctor assured him, leaning in closer to Bens arm.

"Is it broken?" Ben asked. He actually sounded hopeful. "I want a cast to wear to school."

"It is broken. See, right here?" The doctor held up the x-ray to the light showing the fracture in the photo. Ben stared at it, impressed that his bone was in a picture. Dr. Carl looked at me.

"How bad is it?" I asked. It didn't look that bad on the x-ray, but I knew absolutely nothing about broken bones.

"It's just a fracture, nothing to be too worried about. We'll have to put it in a cast, but he'll be healed up in about six weeks." Dr. Carl lowered the x-ray from the light. "Luckily, it doesn't look like there was any nerve damage."

I let out a sigh, glad there was nothing seriously wrong with my baby.

"I'll have the nurse come in, and we'll start putting the cast on…." He stopped as Cee walked in.

"Oh, hey Cee, I haven't seen you in a while," the doctor greeted him. "How do you know this nice young man?"

"Hi, Dr. Carl. I actually nanny for him." Cee smiled. "How is he?"

"I was just explaining to them that the x-ray came back good. A slight fracture, but nothing major. It doesn't look like there was any nerve damage."

Cee smiled, and he seemed to relax a bit at the news. "That's really good."

"I was just about to head out and grab the nurse so we can start putting the cast on," the doctor informed him.

"Thanks, Doc. I really appreciate your help." Cee held out his hand.

"Not a problem," the doctor replied, shaking Cee's hand like an old friend. "By the way, how is your sister doing? I haven't seen her in a while."

Cee's eyes darted to me. He swallowed hard. I couldn't help but have a shocked expression. He had a sister! How did I not know this?

Cee's eyes went back to the doctor. "She's good. She's actually up on the orthopedic floor. She had her last surgery a few months ago, and she's been in physical therapy for the last few weeks. I'll tell her you say hi."

"That would be great. You four take care," the doctor said, stepping back and closing the curtain behind him. Cee walked over to me. I still had my jaw on the floor.

"You have a sister?" Ben asked, breaking the silence. "I didn't know that. Why haven't I met her?"

"Yes, I have a sister," Cee explained. "She's older than you, she's twelve years old, and she's been in the hospital for a long time."

"What happened?" Ben asked.

"Well…" Cee took a deep breath. It was obviously something that he wasn't quite ready to explain.

Luckily for him, right at at that moment, Rachel walked in with the equipment to put Ben's arm in the cast. Cee took a seat next to me, watching as she plastered Ben's arm up. She talked to Ben, explaining each step as she did it. It all turned into a giant blur and I did my best to wipe my eyes without being too obvious.

"Now, what color do you want?" Rachel asked, holding up a selection.

"Green!" Ben announced with a giant grin.

"Green's my favorite too." Rachel whispered. She smiled and began doing the final wrap. I was itching with questions for Cee, but didn't want to take my attention away from Ben. Rachel finally finished up the last steps and looked at Ben.

"All done. Now, remember, you can't get this wet for a while, and it will itch," Rachel warned. "I'll give your mom this packet of instructions of what to do. Make sure to listen to her about it, okay?"

Ben nodded.

"Are we able to go?" I asked as she handed me the packet.

"Not yet, we still have to observe Ben for a few hours," she explained. "You said he hit his head pretty hard, and we want to make sure he doesn't have a concussion."

I nodded, annoyed that we were stuck here for a few more hours. But things could be worse.

My phone started buzzing.

"Hey Jes. I'm here," Richard's voice came through the phone and made me wince. "Where are you guys?"

"We're in the back, and Ben just finished getting his wrist wrapped. I'll come grab you." I walked through the maze of hallways my head still spinning from the revelation of Cee having a sister. I opened the double doors to find Richard standing still, but tapping his foot impatiently.

"What happened?" Richard asked, concern filling his voice.

"He ran away from Cindy's," I explained. "We went out looking for him and found him at a playground. He had fallen off his bike and hurt his wrist. They took him in for X-rays and said he had a slight fracture. He just got a cast."

As soon as Richard saw Ben sitting on the examination

table watching TV, he rushed over and gave him a huge hug. Ben held up his cast to show his dad how awesome it was. I smiled, glad that Ben was still excited, even if it was promptly followed by a yawn.

"Hey, I'm going to get something with caffeine. You guys want anything?" I asked.

Richard and Ben shook their heads and continued their conversation about how the cast was put on. Cee stood up.

"I'll show you where the good stuff is." He grabbed my shoulder lightly and guided me away. I nearly shied away, but instead just kept walking.

"I wanted to talk to you real quick," he said as we stepped out. "I know you were shocked to find out about my sister."

We stopped in a hallway and he turned his body to face mine. Being alone with him was making my heart pound. I wasn't ready to be alone with him yet.

"I didn't realize you had a sister, or that she was in the hospital. Why didn't you ever tell me?" I asked, the hurt filling my voice. First he was cheating, and now he was lying about his family.

"I didn't want to tell you about her. I don't tell anyone about her." He glanced at me, sighing, "I'm the reason she's here." The words came out as a whisper. Cee's eyes met mine, and I could see the guilt.

"Because of you?" I stared at him, trying to understand. "How is that even possible?"

"I was in college. It was my senior year on scholarship," He explained. I nodded, remembering that he had told me this before. "I'd been getting bad grades, and the school threatened to take it away."

"I remember you telling me that," I said slowly.

"My parents drove up from Arizona with my sister to talk to me about it. I'd been ignoring their calls and not taking their threats of taking me home seriously. It wasn't until they knocked on my apartment door that I had realized they made the drive." He took a big breath in, I could see it shake his shoulders. "I got mad, told them I didn't care. I was an adult and I could do what I wanted." He dropped his gaze from me and looked at his feet. "It was so stupid."

"Cee..." I wished I had something to say. He held up his hand to let him finish.

"My dad was pissed, my mom started crying. I know they wanted the best for me, but at the time, I didn't care what they wanted. They drove back to the hotel that they were staying at the next town over. Cheaper rates then ones nearby apparently. It was raining that night, and I guess the tires on the car were bald."

Cee paused, his face haunted and cut with grief. I reached out and put my hand on his shoulder, feeling him shake beneath my fingers.

"My father lost control and went into oncoming traffic. I got the call from the hospital, saying my sister was there. I rushed over to find my sister in a coma and that both of my parents had been killed on impact." He stared off into the distance, replaying the nightmare memory in his mind. "The only reason my sister survived was because she was in the back seat. She was in the ICU for months. I dropped out of school and tried to be with her for every second of it. All the surgeries, all the pain..."

I could see how hard it was for him to admit this. I grabbed his hand, and he looked up at me. I saw his eyes water with tears. "I'm so sorry, Cee..." I whispered.

"I'm sorry... I haven't told anyone this before," he whispered, his voice cracking. I squeezed his hand, waiting for him to continue. I felt a tear trickle down my own cheek. "When she finally woke up, they said her back was broken.

She would be bound to a wheelchair for life." His voice choked. "I transferred her to Grace Hospital because it's one of the best pediatric hospitals in California. I visit her almost every day. She is here because of me. I can never forgive myself for that.

"Oh, Cee..." I squeezed his hand again. I didn't have any words that could make him feel any better.

"That's why I never told you about her." He took a jagged breath in, his eyes searching my face for forgiveness. "I'm ashamed of what I did."

He stopped talking, taking deep raspy breaths in. I gave him a hug. We stood there and just held each other in our arms. I kept wiping away my tears on my shoulder. I couldn't believe he had to deal with so much. It explained why he acted so much older than his age. He inhaled deeply and took a step back.

"I've wanted you to meet her for a while now, but just didn't know how to tell you." His voice was still raw with emotion. "We had gotten so far in our relationship, and I was so worried that if I told you, I would break your trust. I know how hard it is for you to trust people. "

"What's her name?" I asked after a moment.

"Ann."

My heart sunk, it had dawned on me who he had been texting all along, not another woman named Ann, but his sister.

"Her real name is Ryann. My parents had a sense of humor about naming kids. Nothing like having a son named Stacey and a daughter named Ryann." He gave a half-hearted chuckled. I remembered all the texts, and suddenly understood why they said "I love you" and "I miss you."

A chuckle escaped my lips. I don't know why that was the emotion that came out, but it did. I felt it taking control of me, rocking my body. Cee stepped away, looking at me concerned. "Are you okay?"

"I'm such a bitch," was all that I could sputter out between laughs. I shook my head, overwhelmed.

"I thought you were cheating on me with an Ann. I read all those texts, and saw all the phone calls." Tears were streaming down my face, I was so happy, so angry and so relieved that I didn't know what else to do but laugh and cry.

Cee continued to stare at me puzzled, trying to comprehend what was so funny. When I was finally able to get myself under control, I looked up at Cee and he was grinning from ear to ear.

It took him a moment to realize what had finally clicked in my brain. He wasn't cheating on me at all, and I wasn't mad anymore. He grabbed me and kissed me on the lips. It was exactly what I needed. I could feel the heat rise in my cheeks, better than a blush or a glow. He released me from his lips, but still held on to me.

"I'm sorry, sorry for everything," he said, his hands strong on my back. "I should have told you from the beginning that Ann was my sister. Whenever I got a call from Grace, it was from the hospital, this hospital, to let me know how she was doing."

Cee stared at me with his dark eyes. "I wanted to tell you as soon as you saw those messages, but you were so angry. I didn't have a chance. I should have told you sooner. I can understand if you are still mad at me. I kept something big from you." He released me from his arms and straightened up. I grabbed his hand and looked up at him.

"I understand." I smiled up at him. He was such a good man. "You love your sister. You protect her. Just promise me this..."

"Anything."

"Never keep anything from me again."

"I promise, as long as you do me one thing," he replied.

"What?" I clinked, unsure of what he would ask.

"Never keep this from me." He touched my chest above my heart. I felt it skip a beat.

"It's yours," I whispered. I meant it. He deserved my heart. And with that, I leaned in and kissed him.

CHAPTER 31

"Would you like to meet her?" Cee asked.

"Of course, but is it too late?" I wasn't sure how much time had passed in the ER, but it was well past ten, I knew that much.

"No worries. I also have an in with the nursing staff." He winked and grabbed my hand. "Besides, it'll give Ben some time to show his cast off to Richard."

We walked through the winding halls of the hospital. I was expecting the standard white walls and white floors, but I was surprised. There was artwork hanging from the walls of bright flowers, or cartoon characters. The floors had feet painted on it directing you where to go. The cheeriness of the atmosphere made me wish that adult hospitals were more like this.

We finally found ourselves at the orthopedic entrance. We walked through the double doors to a receptionist desk. Typing on their computers were two nurses, and one looked up from the computer as we approached.

"Cee! How are you doing? We normally don't get to see you anymore on this shift." The nurse stood up and gave him a hug. She was a cute older woman, with blond hair and kind blue eyes. She smiled at me. "And who might this be?"

"This is my…" He looked at me, not wanting to introduce me wrong.

"Girlfriend, Jes." I held out my hand.

"Oh, so you're the one who he won't shut up about. So glad to meet you." She shook my hand. "Many of the nurses were mad that you took this handsome guy off the market."

I smiled, and looked at Cee.

"Can we go see Ann?" I asked the nurse.

"Sure, they just finished up a movie. You'll find her in her room. Don't stay too late. You know how much Agnes hates it if you keep her up." The nurse walked back around the desk and sat down. Cee grabbed my hand and led me up the hallway.

"Agnes?" I looked at Cee.

"She's the morning nurse. She likes to have people up in the morning and she gets upset when I keep Ann up late. Ann isn't exactly a morning person."

As we walked along the hall, many of the doors were open, but the rooms were darkened. I could hear the soft murmur of televisions, and the beep of machines. I passed by one room and saw a kid laying in his hospital bed, fast asleep. His sheets were decorated with super heroes, just like the ones Ben wanted.

The thought of Ben being up here broke my heart.

We turned to the last door in the hall and knocked. Cee pushed the door open to find Ann laying on her bed. The room was covered in drawings, and pictures of her and Cee. She had dark purple sheets with white stitching. She looked like any other twelve-year-old girl tucked into bed, and if I hadn't seen the IV poles and machines, I would have thought it was a typical room.

The first thing I noticed about her was her red hair. It was fiery red with natural streaks of blond in it, exactly opposite of Cee's. It framed her pale face and stood out against the white pillowcase she was laying on.

"Cee, I didn't think you were going to come tonight." She held out her arms for a hug. I saw Cee melt to that smile as he walked over and gave her a giant bear hug. I faced into the wall, not wanting to disturb their time.

"We had an unexpected visit to the ER with Ben. He broke his arm. Dr. Carl actually took care of him. Do you remember him?" They broke off into chatter about Dr. Carl, and the stupid jokes he used to tell to make Ann feel better.

I stood by the door, entranced watching their interaction together. Cee almost became another person. His body language was more relaxed and there was a twinkle in his eye that I had never seen before.

Ann's eyes flickered over to me and Cee stopped talking. "I wanted you to meet someone while we're here." He held out my hand so that I would walk towards them. "This is Jes." Ann's eyes lit up, and she gave me a huge smile.

"You're Jes! I'm so glad to meet you." She held out her arms for a hug. I smiled at the greeting and walked over, happy to oblige. I wrapped my arms around her and felt her strong grip as she wrapped me in her arms. She was stronger than she looked.

"Hi, it's so great to meet you too," I said after being released from her arms. I was at a loss for words to say anything else.

"He didn't tell you about me, did he?" She looked over at Cee, giving him a disapproving pout. For being just twelve years old, she sure did have some attitude.

"No, he just told me about you a few minutes ago," I admitted, glancing bashfully at Cee.

"STACEY JOAN COOK," Ann chastised in a serious

voice. I couldn't help but giggle. She sounded just like a mother.

"Ryann Oscar Cook," he teased back.

"Don't call me Ryann. You know I hate that." She made a gag face.

"Then don't call me Stacey and make up crazy middle names." He looked at me. "Joan is not my middle name. She just likes to make up ridiculous middle names to tease me."

I laughed. Just watching them showed they were true siblings who really cared about one another. I heard a knock on the door. It was the nurse who'd greeted us at the station.

"Hey, sorry to interrupt, but visiting hours are really over. And you..." She pointed her finger at Ann, "...have physical therapy tomorrow. I don't want Agnes getting on my case again for letting you stay up late."

"But Mary, this is my first time meeting Jes." She pouted her lower lip and gave big puppy dog eyes.

"Nope, that will not work on me tonight. Say goodbye." She covered her eyes to avoid the look Ann continued to give her as she walked out of sight.

"It was a pleasure meeting you, Ann." I hugged her one last time.

"Glad to meet you, too. Please come visit again soon. I'd love to have a girl to talk to. Cee doesn't like to talk about boys, or hair, or really anything that I like to talk about." She rolled her eyes at his exasperated sigh, but smiled when Cee bent over and gave her a final hug goodbye.

"She will be back, that I promise you." He kissed her on the forehead and pulled the sheets up.

"Good, I want to try some of her spicy French toast you were talking about." She gave me a final wink.

"Goodnight, Ann," Cee said, exasperated.

"She is adorable," I said, taking his hand as we walked down the hallway.

"I'm glad you like her. She really likes you." He grinned at me as he gave a slight wave to the nurses at the station on our way back to the ER.

Things were falling back into place. I was actually smiling by the time we got back to where Richard and Ben were waiting to be discharged. Richard looked up from his phone.

"The nurse came back, it looks like we're okay to leave. Ben isn't exhibiting any concussion symptoms." Richard sounded as relieved as I felt. "We're ready to go when you are."

"You ready to go home?" I held my hand out to Ben.

He grabbed it, and I helped him up.

"Yes." He yawned at me. The bags under his eyes suggested that he was ready to go home. "But where did you guys go?"

"We visited Cee's sister," I responded.

"And you didn't take me? I want to meet her, too!" Ben tried to sound angry, but a yawn cut him off mid-sentence.

"You were a little busy," I reminded him. "We'll meet her again. Just ask Cee."

"I promise you'll get to meet my sister, Ben. Now let's get you home."

We got him back into some clean clothes that Richard had brought, and made our way out to the car. Richard gave Ben one last hug.

"I'll talk to you tomorrow, okay? Let me know if you need anything." He stood up and looked at me.

"Let me know if you need anything as well." He gave me an awkward hug and walked to his car. I stared after him, feeling a strange happiness in my chest. We weren't partners anymore, but at least he was treating me as an equal.

Cee got Ben in his seat, and made sure he was secure. Ben already was dozing as soon as he was clicked in.

The ride back was quiet and uneventful. Cee carried Ben

up to his bed and I tucked him in quietly. I stayed for an extra moment, just watching his chest rise and fall, lifting the green cast up and down. I was beyond glad that he was okay.

We walked back downstairs and I collapsed onto the couch. I closed my eyes for a moment, trying to remember the events of the day and how everything flew by. I felt the cushion beside me indent as he sat down. He put his hand on my head and slowly stroked my hair.

I couldn't believe so much had happened. I had started out my day hating this man, and lying to my son. Now, I had my son tucked into bed with a broken arm, and the man I was afraid I had lost forever was sitting there stroking my hair.

"How are you feeling?" Cee asked. His voice was soothing and wonderful.

"Exhausted. Stupid. I should've listened to you. Should've," I murmured, feeling myself drift off to sleep while he continued to play with my hair. I opened my eyes. "I have to take you home. I just remembered that I picked you up."

"Don't worry about it." He continued to brush back my hair. I couldn't fight sleep any longer and I closed my eyes. "Don't worry about any of it."

I slept like a rock. I hadn't slept this good in days. I woke up feeling rested. I stretched and opened my eyes to see my bedroom. I didn't remember falling asleep in my bedroom. I checked the clock, it was already eight o'clock, and I was late for work. My cell phone was not in its normal spot, and I ran downstairs, frantic to find it. My boss was going to be pissed.

"Have you seen my cell phone, I'm late for work and need to call in," I asked Cee as I ran to the couch, trying to find the damn phone.

"This?" He waved my phone in the air.

"YES!" I hurried over and reached out my hand.

"I hope you don't mind, but I called your office this morning," Cee said, dropping it in my outstretched palm. "I let them know what happened to Ben last night. They said to take the day to make sure he's all right."

I smiled, instantly relaxing. He really did think of everything, and I was so thankful my job had been understanding. I was going to be a model employee after this.

"Thank you." I went over and gave him a hug. "How did I get to bed last night?"

"I carried you, then I slept on the couch. I wanted to make sure that if you or Ben needed me, I was here." He hugged me tight. "I checked on him a few times last night, and he was sound asleep."

"Wow. You're the best," I told him.

"Cee, you're here!" Ben shouted as he jumped the last two steps. He lost his balance slightly, forgetting that one arm was a bit heavier than the other.

"Yes he is, and I took the day off," I informed Ben with a hug. "How are you feeling?"

"Good. Everything kind of hurts, though." He rubbed his knee where there were scabs forming.

I looked at Ben and frowned. He was still in his clothes from last night. We'd been too tired to get him in his pajamas. I laughed as I touched his face. He even still had some dirt on his face from when he fell.

"We'll get you some breakfast, and then we'll get you in the bath and clean you all up," I said.

"Moooom, I can do it myself." He frowned at me like a little teenager.

I laughed. "Let's see how well you can eat your breakfast with one hand, and then talk to me about the bath."

Cee had a breakfast of toast, eggs and bacon ready for us in no time. Nothing too fancy, but delicious and perfect for what we needed. We watched as Ben tried to butter his toast with one hand, giggling at him as he was unwilling to ask for help. He continued to stab through his toast with his knife. It wasn't until his third failed attempt that he finally looked at me.

"Alright, can I have some help?" He refused to make eye contact.

"Of course," I assured him. "You did a decent job. You'll get better at it."

I grabbed the butter and jam and made him a slice of toast. We ate in silence, still waking up from our long nights. When we cleared off the last piece of bacon, we started to clear the dishes. Ben brought over things one at a time, learning how to use his non-dominant hand for things.

We started on the next task, getting Ben to take a bath. Luckily Cee had broken a few arms in his childhood, and helped Ben with everything. At about noon the door rang, and Richard was there with lunch.

"Hi, sorry to stop over unannounced. I just wanted to see how everyone is doing." Richard smiled nervously. "I brought food."

He brought in the bags of food and laid out the sandwiches and chips he brought. Ben came over and talked to his dad some more, reassuring him that everything was okay.

We ate lunch together, laughing at Ben as he tried to open a bag of chips and instead making the bag explode and flinging chips everywhere. After we polished off all of the food, Richard headed back to work so Ben could lay down to watch some TV while Cee and I cleaned up.

"Cee, thank you again for everything," I said while tossing the trash away. "I really appreciate it. I'm glad too to have some time to talk with you."

Cee placed the last dish in the dishwasher and looked at me. "Me too."

"So, you know Ben starts school next week, and I really

don't need a nanny anymore," I said slowly. Cee's body tensed up at the words, so I quickly continued. "So I was wondering, if instead of being my son's nanny, would you be my boyfriend?" I could feel the cheesiness of the words as they left my lips.

"Ah, finally, my sense of romance has rubbed off on you." He got closer to me, pulling me in. He leaned in and gave me a kiss.

"That's not an answer," I retorted, but secretly loving it. He kissed me again.

"If you want me as your boyfriend, I'll have to get some paperwork for us to fill out, expectations, and time frames. I mean, I do have things to do." He chuckled and gave me another kiss.

EPILOGUE

"*D*o I look okay?" I turned around in my short white dress, and all the girls oo-ed and ahh-ed at it. I had kept things very simple. I opted for a strapless tea length gown with accents of pearls and lace around the bodice. My hair was gently curled, falling around my shoulders and accented with a flower at my ear.

"You look fantastic!" Cindy assured me, giving me a hug.

"Absolutely wonderful!" Melissa agreed, holding up her glass of champagne to "cheers" at me.

"It's almost time to go," Tracy interrupted, pointing at her watch.

"Are you ready for this?" Ann asked. She sat in her wheelchair nearby.

"Okay." I took a big breath in and started to follow everyone out the door. As I walked toward the door, I remembered how quickly time seemed to have flown by.

Two years since Cee walked into my life.

Each day was better than the last. I couldn't believe that each day I could fall more in love with someone.

After about six months together, and a lot of begging

from me, he finally moved in with Ben and me. I wanted to have him around all the time. I also wanted him to stop being a nanny and do something he really wanted to do. I wanted him to pursue his dream of becoming a chef.

Ann wheeled herself by and grabbed my hand. "What are you thinking about?" she asked. I smiled down at her. "I was just remembering how Cee proposed to me." I chuckled fondly at the memory.

Cee had just graduated school and we were having an amazing dinner to celebrate. After we stuffed ourselves silly, he brought out some black forest brownies. It had easily become my favorite dessert ever since he introduced it to me.

Ben and I greedily ate our dessert, polishing off our plates in no time. We looked up at Cee and saw that he'd barely touched his plate. Each bite he would look at, place it in his mouth, slowly swallow and then nod his head, as if each bite was a completely different taste. Ben and I sat in silence as we watched Cee take his sweet time.

I heard his phone buzz and he checked it.

"Hey, I just got a text from Cindy, she wants us to come over for a game night in celebration of me finishing school. Do you want to go?" Cee asked. He was only halfway done with his dessert.

"Sure. We haven't had a night with her in forever," I agreed.

As if by magic, Cee made the rest of his brownie disappear and quickly put all the dishes into the sink. I sat dumbfounded at the sudden switch. It was if Cee suddenly remembered that he had the ability to move at a rate faster than turtle's pace.

We grabbed our shoes and headed out the door to a warm

night. Ben scampered ahead of us and made it to Cindy's house before we even got to the sidewalk. I saw his body dart in through the door and he left it ajar in his excitement. I shook my head and quickly walked to catch up with Cee right beside me. I didn't want all of her air-conditioning to escape.

We made it inside, and I made sure the door was securely closed behind me. As soon as I got into the kitchen, I felt like all eyes were on me. It was a much bigger game night than I expected. Cindy and Tricia were sitting around the table with Melissa. Ray, Cindy's husband, was standing getting drinks filled. I smiled as I walked in, feeling as though I was missing out on some sort of secret.

"I had no idea you guys were here, too. It's so great to see you." I went around giving out hugs.

"Since you got that big promotion we never get to see you anymore," Melissa said, hugging her arms around me.

"Yeah, it has been a bit crazy, I still can't believe they picked me." I walked to the table and sat down on an empty chair. "Where is Ben?" I looked around, seeing Jake sitting on the couch watching a movie.

"Oh, he's just grabbing something from upstairs," Melissa replied, waving a nonchalant hand through the air.

"Okay, what are we playing tonight?" I asked.

"I think dominoes sound good?" Cindy offered.

"Yeah, sounds fun," I agreed.

At that moment, I heard the scampering of little paws and saw a black lab puppy skittering across the wood floor and Ben chasing after it.

"Who is this little guy?" I said bending over to pick him up. "Did you get a dog?" I looked at Cindy.

She beamed back at me and shook her head. I started to see tears well up in her eyes. I looked at everyone else with the same question and they all shook their heads "no" as well.

I grabbed the pink collar that was around the wiggling ball of fur. Between wet kisses, I found the silver tag shaped like a heart. On one side it had "Cee and Jes" engraved. I flipped it over to the other side, and inscribed was "Will you marry me?" I froze in shock. I felt the squirming dog get pulled out of my hands, and my view was no longer obscured.

"You always said you wanted a dog." Cee was on one knee with a ring box open in one of his hands. "Jes, I love you. The time that we have spent together has been amazing. I never want to spend a moment without you."

He pulled the ring out of the box and grabbed my shaking left hand.

"Will you marry me?" He asked, his violet eyes enveloped me.

"Yes, yes of course!" I yelled. I bent over and hugged him, tears streaming down my face. I heard a cheer erupt and looked around to everyone. Cindy was dabbing her eyes and Ben gave the thumbs up, the puppy squirming in his arms.

"But really, whose dog is this?" I asked as Ben put the puppy down and it ran across the floor. Everyone chuckled

"It's yours, mom!" Ben giggled.

"You coming, Jes?" Cindy called out. I had fallen behind, lost in thought. I ran down the hallway to catch up to everyone.

I had made the decision not to have any bridesmaids, but wanted them to know that if I did, it would be them.

I wanted this day to be about me, Cee and our love.

I did have a maid of honor though – Ann. She moved in with us a few months ago, after being discharged from the hospital, and we were fast friends. Our bond grew thanks to the hours we spent at physical therapy.

We made our way out from the hotel and onto the beach. I got behind Ann and helped her push her chair as the wheels stuck easily in the sand. I was very glad I'd opted for a short dress and sandals as the sand whipped around my feet.

We arrived to find everyone standing on the beach. It was a small party, just family and close friends. Cee and I wanted a short ceremony and thought chairs were useless.

I stood next to Ann as I watched each of my friends walk down the aisle, and take their seats. I patted Ann on the shoulder and pushed her to the aisle marked out in tea-light candles. Cee had his back to us, and he was looking out to the ocean.

I was glad I had made him face away so as to not catch a glimpse. He was dressed in a gray suit. Next to him was Ben in an identical suit, looking amazing. He held the leash of the black lab, Dinger, who had a pink bow-tie around his neck. I gave Ben a slight nod and waited as Ben gave Cee the signal to turn around. His smile was so big that I could see every tooth at the end of the aisle. He took my breath away. I quickly sniffed and tried to keep the tears at bay. I leaned down to Ann and whispered in her ear, "You ready for the water works?"

"Yes."

I held out my arm. She took a firm grip and slowly helped raised herself up to a standing position. She gave me a little nod, and I took a step and she followed suit. Everyone let out a small gasp.

She was walking, something that doctors had told us she would never do again. She took another small step, leaning slightly. I tried to take as much weight as I could as we took each step, knowing that each movement of her legs was exhausting. I looked up at Cee. Tears were running down his face. He wasn't paying attention to them, but watching us take each step.

I whispered to her as we took a few more steps, "You are so mean, wanting to make your big brother cry, especially in photos."

She nodded her head, focusing on each step, but she gave me a devilish grin. She had decided after we had gotten engaged to make it her goal to walk down the aisle. When I visited her one day in the hospital, she told me what she wanted to do, and how she wanted to keep it a secret.

I came by once a week and worked with her. She had a renewed vigor about the therapy. We made it down the aisle, and Cee gave her a big hug, his cheeks wet with tears.

"Why didn't you tell me about this?" His voice cracked with emotion.

"We wanted to surprise you." Ann gave him a kiss on the cheek as if what she did was no large feat. I helped her back into the wheelchair that had been brought up by one of the crowd. I could tell she was tired.

"You did so well! He was definitely shocked." I gave her a kiss on the check.

"You look beautiful. Now, go get married to my brother." Ann smiled.

I stood up and looked to Cee, his eyes still wet with tears. I grinned. It was so great to see a man who had such emotion. I walked to him and he grabbed my hands. The officiate took control of the ceremony, and led us through our vows.

"Do you, Jes, take Cee to be you husband?" he asked.

"I do," I vowed.

"And Cee, do you take Jes to be your wife?"

"I do," he promised.

"Then with the power vested in me by the state of California, I pronounce you man and wife. You may kiss your bride."

Cee and I leaned in for our kiss. I felt his lips on mine,

and his arms wrapped around me. It was official, I was married to my nanny.

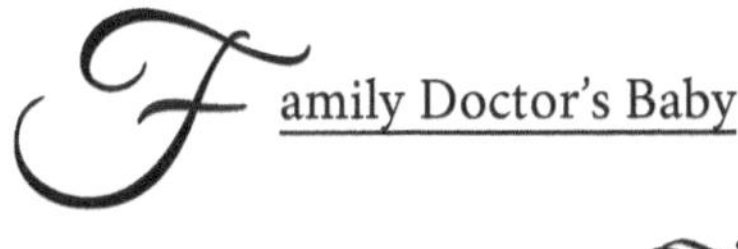

amily Doctor's Baby

From New York Times bestselling author Krista Lakes, comes a sexy standalone novel about the baddest bad boy doctor and the sweet little nurse that he falls for.

When I left my small hometown years ago, I never expected to come back. I certainly never expected that when I did, I'd be working for *him*.

He's the town's doctor. He's supposed to be a respectable member of society, a pillar for the community. He's supposed to have come a long way from the bad boy who rode a motorcycle in high school.

But he hasn't. One glance from those lustful eyes looking at me tells me that he has the same voracious appetites that he did when we were younger.

Only it's not quite the same stare. It's more urgent. It's more intense. I'm not the same nerdy girl who tutored him.

I've grown up, developed fertile curves that I know he finds irresistible.

In this small town, rumors travel fast, and the family doctor can't be seen as a player. So he does try to resist. And I do too. But with every smoldering glance and moment of sexual tension, we find our barriers breaking down.

After a stressful night of touch-and-go baby delivery, a moment of elation overcomes our inhibitions. It seems like maybe we'll need to confront those rumors sooner rather than later, especially before I begin to show the results of that night.

Can I give this doctor the family he has always desired?

Dr. Matthews leaned in and brought his lips toward mine. He paused right before our lips touched. Just for a moment, though. It was as if he were making sure that I wanted this. The universe held its breath as we both held our breath. I noticed everything from the way his aftershave lingered in the air to the water droplets in his hair. After a second that felt like eternity, he leaned in the rest of the way, firmly pressing his lips against mine.

Our fate was sealed.

A soft moan made its way up my throat as I relaxed into his kiss. I closed my eyes and let my hands drift up toward his face. His beard stubble tickled my fingertips as I dragged them over his cheeks.

It must have been the adrenaline we'd both experienced that morning. Or maybe it was that the emergency had bonded us closer than ever before. I didn't know what had gotten into either of us, but I suppose it didn't need explaining. It felt good and right and that's all I really cared about. I needed a release that only he could give me.

Jacob slowly broke our kiss and dropped his hands to the top of my hips. Then he leaned in again, passionately pressing his lips to mine. My heart began to do flip flops behind my rib cage. Within a few seconds, I felt Jacob open his mouth and gently dart his tongue out, teasing it into my mouth.

A tingling sensation coursed through my body as our tongues lightly wrestled with each others, twisting around in a sensual dance. I reveled in the sensations: his taste, his smell, the way he held his body against mine. This wasn't a dream. This was actually happening.

Jacob broke the kiss and took a step back. His cheeks were flushed and his eyes dark.

"I'm sorry. That was unprofessional."

My heart hammered in my chest and my lips ached for more of his kisses.

"I don't care," I told him. "I don't want to stop."

He looked up, his eyes bright as they met mine. Desire that matched my own shone in them and my body heated. I took the step forward to bring us back together. Slowly, I brought my hand up and wrapped it around the back of his neck.

"Are you sure you're okay with this?" he asked, his hands already coming to my hips.

"Just shut up and kiss me," I said, still smiling.

<u>Family Doctor's Baby</u>

An Endless Kind of Love

Billionaires and Brides
    Yours Completely: A Cinderella Love Story
    Yours Truly: A Cinderella Love Story
    Yours Royally: A Cinderella Love Story

The "Kisses" series
    Saltwater Kisses: A Billionaire Love Story
    Kisses From Jack: The Other Side of Saltwater Kisses
    Rainwater Kisses: A Billionaire Love Story
    Champagne Kisses: A Timeless Love Story
    Freshwater Kisses: A Billionaire Love Story
    Sandcastle Kisses: A Billionaire Love Story
    Hurricane Kisses: A Billionaire Love Story
    Barefoot Kisses: A Billionaire Love Story
    Sunrise Kisses: A Billionaire Love Story
    Waterfall Kisses: A Billionaire Love Story
    Island Kisses: A Billionaire Love Story

Other Novels
    I Choose You: A Secret Billionaire Romance
    His Every Desire: A Billionaire Seduction
    Wolf Six's Salvation: A Shifter Love Story
    Burned: A New Adult Love Story
    Walking on Sunshine: A Sweet Summer Romance
    An American Cinderella: A Royal Love Story
    Mr. Darcy's Kiss: A Contemporary Pride and Prejudice

www.ingramcontent.com/pod-product-compliance
Lightning Source LLC
Chambersburg PA
CBHW050352190726
48284CB00007BB/2256